M. GORKY

TALES OF ITALY

М. Горький

M. GORKY

TALES OF ITALY

Fredonia Books
Amsterdam, The Netherlands

Tales of Italy

by
M. Gorky

ISBN: 1-58963-527-2

Reprinted from the original edition

Fredonia Books
Amsterdam, the Netherlands
http://www.fredoniabooks.com

CONTENTS

TALES OF ITALY

*"There are no tales finer
than those created by life itself.*

HANS ANDERSEN

THE STRIKE

THE TRAM-CAR employees in Naples were on strike:
a string of empty cars stretched the entire length of
the Riviera di Chiaia and a crowd of conductors and
drivers, jolly, voluble Neapolitans, as volatile as quick-
silver, had gathered on Piazza della Vittoria. Above their
heads over the park fence sparkled a fountain jet like the
slender blade of a sword, around them pressed a large,
hostile crowd of people who had to travel on business
to all parts of the huge city and all these shop assistants,
artisans, tradesmen and seamstresses loudly reproached
the strikers. Harsh words and biting jibes were exchanged
and there was much gesticulating, for the Neapolitans

11

speak as expressively and eloquently with their hands as with their indefatigable tongues.

A light breeze wafted from the sea, the dark green fronds of the tall palms in the city park swayed gently, their trunks looking strangely like the clumsy legs of some monster elephants. Urchins, the half-naked children of the Neapolitan streets, romped about, filling the air with their sparrow-like twitter and laughter.

The city, which resembled an old engraving, was bathed in the generous rays of the blazing sun and seemed to reverberate like an organ; the blue waves in the gulf plashed against the stone embankment adding a muffled beat, like the throbbing of a tambourine, to the hubbub and cries of the city.

The strikers huddled gloomily together, barely replying to the irritable outcries of the crowd; some of them climbed on to the railing of the park peering anxiously down the street over the heads of the people, like a pack of wolves surrounded by the hounds. It was clear that these people in their uniformed attire were closely linked by an unshakable resolve to stand their ground, and this irritated the crowd still more. But the crowd had its philosophers. Smoking calmly, they admonished the more impassioned opponents of the strikers thus:

"Ah, signor! What is a man to do if he can't afford macaroni for his children?"

Sprucely attired agents of the municipal police stood by in groups of two and three to see that the crowd did not obstruct the movement of the carriages. They kept strictly neutral, regarding with like equanimity the censurers and censured and good-humouredly chaffing both sides when shouts and gestures became too heated. A detachment of carabinieri carrying their short, light rifles were lined up against the buildings on a narrow side-street, ready to intervene in the event of serious clashes. They made a rather sinister group in their three-cornered hats, abbreviated capes and the scarlet stripes like two streaks of blood running down their trousers.

Suddenly the wrangling, jeers, reproaches and persuasions subsided. Some new spirit swept the crowd, a pacifying spirit it seemed; the strikers moved closer together with set faces as a shout went up from the crowd:

"The soldiers!"

Whistles of mockery and triumph directed at the strikers mingled with shouts of greeting and one stout man in a light-grey suit and a panama hat broke into a caper, tapping with his feet against the stone causeway.

The conductors and drivers made their way slowly through the crowd to the cars, some climbed aboard.

They looked grimmer than before as they forced their way through the crowd snapping retorts to the exclamations from all sides. The hubbub subsided.

Up from the Santa Lucia embankment with a light, dancing step came the little grey soldiers, their feet beating a rhythmic tattoo and their left hands swinging with a mechanical motion. They looked like tin soldiers and as fragile as toys. They were led by a tall handsome officer with knit brows and a contemptuous twist to his lips; beside him hopped a stout man in a top hat chattering volubly and cleaving the air with innumerable gestures.

The crowd fell back from the cars; the soldiers scattered like so many grey beads, taking up positions at the platforms of the cars where the strikers stood.

The man in the top hat and several other respectable-looking citizens around him waved their arms wildly and shouted:

"The last time... ultima volta! Do you hear?"

The officer stood with his head inclined twirling his moustache with a bored air; the man ran up to him waving his top hat and shouting something in a hoarse voice. The officer glanced at him out of the corner of his eye, then drew himself up, threw out his chest and rapped out commands in a loud voice.

Whereupon the soldiers began jumping on to the platforms of the cars, two on each platform, while the drivers and conductors jumped down one after the other.

This struck the crowd as funny—it roared, whistled and laughed, but all at once the noise subsided and with grim, tense faces and eyes wide with horror the people fell back from the cars in heavy silence, and pressed towards the front car.

There, within two feet of its wheels, stretched across the rails, lay one of the drivers. His grey head was bared and his face, the face of a soldier with the moustaches bristling angrily, stared up at the sky. As the crowd gaped, a lad, small and agile as a monkey, threw himself down beside the driver, and one by one others followed suit.

A low hum rose from the crowd and voices were heard calling fearfully on the Madonna, some cursed grimly, the women screamed and groaned and the urchins jumped up and down in excitement, like rubber balls.

The man in the top hat yelled something in a hysterical voice, the officer looked at him and shrugged his shoulders—his soldiers had been sent to take over the cars from the tram men but he had no orders to fight the strikers.

Then the top hat, surrounded by some obliging citizens, rushed over to the carabinieri-and now they came forward and bent over the men lying on the rails with the intention of removing them.

There was a brief scuffle; then suddenly the whole grey dusty crowd of onlookers swayed, bellowed, howled and rushed over to the rails—the man in the panama snatched off his hat, threw it into the air and was the first to lie down beside the end striker, slapping him on the shoulder and shouting words of encouragement at him.

One by one people began to drop down on to the rails, as if their feet had given way beneath them—jolly, noisy folk who had not been there at all two minutes before. They threw themselves on the ground, laughing and pulling faces at one another and shouting to the officer who was talking to the top-hatted individual, shaking his gloves under his nose with a slight smile, and tossing his handsome head.

More and more people poured on to the rails, women dropped their baskets and bundles, small boys, shaking with laughter, curled up like shivering puppies, and decently dressed people too rolled about in the dust.

The five soldiers standing on the platform of the front car looked down at the heap of bodies under the wheels and roared with laughter, clinging to the bars for support, throwing back their heads and bending forward, convulsed with amusement. They did not look at all like tin soldiers now.

...Half an hour later the tram-cars, scraping and clanging were speeding through the streets of Naples, and on the platforms stood the beaming victors and down the cars walked the victors, asking politely:

"Biglietti?!"

And the passengers handed them red and yellow notes with much winking, smiling and good-natured grumbling.

CHILDREN OF PARMA

ON THE LITTLE square in front of the railway station
in Genoa a dense crowd had gathered, workingmen
for the most part but with a good sprinkling of well-fed,
respectably dressed people as well. In front of the crowd
stood members of the city council; above their heads
waved the heavy and cunningly embroidered silk banner
of the city, with the varicoloured banners of the worker's
organizations beside it. The golden tassels, fringes,
and cords glittered, the tips of the flagpoles shone,
the silk rustled and a low hum like a choir singing
sotto voce rose from the festive throng.

Above, on its tall pedestal, stood the statue of Columbus, the dreamer who had suffered so much for his beliefs and who won because he believed. Today too he looked down at the people and his marble lips seemed to be saying:

"Only those who believe can win."

The musicians had laid their instruments around the pedestal at his feet and the brass glittered like gold in the sun.

The receding semi-circle of the station building spread is heavy marble wings as though wishing to embrace the waiting throng. From the port came the laboured breathing of the steamships, the muffled churning of a propeller in the water, the clanging of chains, whistling and shouting. But the square was still and hot under the broiling sun. On the balconies and at the windows of houses women stood with flowers in their hands and beside them were children looking like flowers in their holiday garb.

As the locomotive rolled whistling into the station the crowd stirred and several crushed hats flew into the air like so many dark birds; the musicians picked up their trumpets, and a few grave, elderly men spruced themselves, hastily stepped forward and turned to face the crowd, speaking excitedly and gesturing to the right and left.

Slowly the crowd parted, clearing a wide passage to the street. "Whom have they come to meet?"

"The children from Parma!"

There was a strike on in Parma. The employers would not yield, and the workers were in such dire straits that they had decided to send their children to Parma to save them from starvation.

From behind the columns of the station building there appeared a neat procession of little people, half-naked and looking like some queer, shaggy little animals in their ragged garments. They walked hand in hand, five abreast, small, dusty and tired. Their faces were grave but their eyes shone brightly, and when the musicians struck up the Garibaldi hymn a smile of pleasure flickered over those gaunt, hunger-pinched little faces.

The crowd welcomed the men and women of the future with a deafening shout, banners dipped before them, the brass trumpets blared out, stunning and dazzling the children; somewhat taken aback by this reception, they shrank back for a moment and then suddenly drew themselves up so that they looked taller, coalesced into a mass and from hundreds of throats there rose a single shout:

"Viva Italia!"

"Long live young Parma!" thundered the crowd, rushing toward them.

"Evviva Garibaldi!" shouted the children, as in a grey wedge they cut into the crowd and were engulfed by it.

In the hotel windows and from the roofs of houses handkerchiefs fluttered like white birds, and a shower of flowers and gay, lively shouts poured down on the heads of the crowd below.

Everything took on a festive appearance, everything sprang to life, even the grey marble seemed to blossom out in daubs of bright colour.

The banners waved in the breeze, caps and flowers flew into the air, the tiny heads of the children rose above the heads of the throng, small grimy paws stretched out in greeting sought to catch the flowers and the air resounded with the mighty, unceasing shout:

"Viva il Socialismo!"

"Evviva Italia!"

Nearly all the children were snatched up, some sat perched on the shoulders of the grown-ups, others were pressed against the broad chests of stern bewhiskered men; the music was barely audible above the hubbub of shouting and laughter.

Women darted in and out of the crowd picking up the remaining newcomers and shouting to one another:

"You'll take two, Annita?"

"Yes. And you?"

"Don't forget one for lame Margaret..."

A feeling of joyous excitement reigned, there were beaming faces and moist kind eyes on all sides, and already some of the striker's children were munching bread.

"No one thought of this in our time!" remarked an old man with a beak-like nose and a black cigar between his teeth.

"And how simple it is..."

"Yes. Simple and sensible."

The old man removed the cigar from his mouth, glanced at its tip and sighed as he shook off the ash. Then noticing two little Parma children—brothers obviously—nearby, he assumed a fierce expression, and while the boys looked on gravely, pushed his hat down over his eyes, spread out his arms and, as the brothers backed away together scowling, suddenly squatted down and crowed like a rooster. The boys roared with laughter, stamping their bare soles on the cobbles; the man rose, straightened his at, and, walked off unsteadily feeling that he had done his duty.

A humpbacked, grey-haired woman, with the face of a witch and wiry grey hairs sprouting on a bony chin, stood at the foot of the statue of Columbus and wept, wiping her reddened eyes with the end of her faded shawl. Dark and ugly, she looked strangely forlorn among the excited throng...

A black-haired young Genoese woman came tripping along, leading by the hand a young man of about seven wearing clogs and a grey hat so large that it reached down almost to his shoulders. He tossed his little head to shake the hat back from his eyes but it kept slipping forward on to his face until the woman swept it off and waved it in the air, laughing and singing; the child, his face wreathed in smiles, threw back his head to look, then jumped up to catch the hat as both disappeared from view.

A tall man with powerful bare arms wearing a leather apron carried a little girl of six on his shoulder, a grey mousey little thing.

"See what I mean?" he remarked to the woman who walked beside him leading a small boy with flaming red hair, "If this sort of thing takes root... it won't be easy to get the better of us, eh?"

And with a deep laugh of triumph he threw his little burden up into the blue air, crying: "Evviva Parma-a!"

The people gradually dispersed carrying the children or leading them by the hand until the square was empty of all save the crumpled flowers, candy wrappers, a group of jolly facchini and over them the noble figure of the man who discovered the New World.

And the happy shouts of the people going forward to a new life echoed through the streets like the flourish of great trumpets.

FLOWERS

It is a sultry noon. The midday gun has just gone off in the distance with a queer muffled sound like the bursting of some giant rotten egg, and in the air, stirred by the explosion, the city odours—the smell of olive oil, garlic, wine and sun-warmed dust—seem more pungent still.

The clamour of the torrid southern day, damped for a moment against the hot stones of the pavement by the dull reverberations of the cannon, rises again over the streets and flows on to the sea in a broad, turbid stream.

The city is as colourful as the richly embroidered

robe of a priest. Its passionate cries, groans and exclamations ring out like a paean to life. Every city is a temple raised by the labours of man, all labour is a prayer to the Future.

The sun is at its zenith and a blinding heat pours down from the blue sky as if every sun ray falling upon earth and sea were a fiery sword thrust into stone and water. The water is like shining silk thickly sewn with silver, its warm green waves lap the shore and it murmurs its gentle hymn to the source of life and happiness—the sun.

Crowds of dusty, sweating men are hurrying to their midday meal, conversing in gay loud voices. Many of them run down to the beach, shed their grimy clothing and plunge into the sea, their bronze bodies absurdly small as they drop into the water, like dark specks of dust in a great bowl of wine.

The silky splash of the water, the joyous cries of the refreshed bathers, the loud laughter and squeals of the children—all this along with the rainbow-hued spray kicked up by many feet rises up to the sun like some gay sacrifice.

On the pavement in the shade of a tall building four navvies, as grey, dry and sturdy as the stones on which they sit, are preparing to dine. With his keen eye narrowed, a greyhaired old man, covered with dust as thick as ashes, is cutting a long loaf, taking care that no slice should be smaller than another. He wears a red knitted cap with a tassel which falls into his eyes, and now and again he tosses his large apostolic head, and the nostrils of his long, parrot-like nose quiver.

A strapping lad with bronze skin and coal-black hair, is sprawled on his back on the hot stones beside him. Crumbs of bread fall on his face and he blinks lazily, humming a tune as if in his sleep. The other two sit leaning against the white walls of the house and dozing.

A boy carrying a fiasca of wine in one hand and a small bundle in the other comes toward them. He throws back his head and shouts something in a voice as shrill as a bird's, unaware that heavy drops of thick ruby-red wine are oozing through the straw encasing the bottle.

But the old man sees it, and laying the bread and the knife on the young man's chest, he waves his hand to the boy and shouts:

"Hurry up, blind one! Look, you're spilling the wine!"

The boy lifts up the fiasca, gasps and runs over quickly to the navvies, who bestir themselves all at once, shouting excitedly and fingering the fiasca, while the boy dashes off into a yard and re-appears at once with a large yellow jug.

He stands the jug on the ground and the old man carefully pours the living red stream into it. Four pairs of eyes lovingly watch the wine sparkling in the sun, and their dry lips quiver.

A woman in a pale blue dress and a gold lace scarf in her black hair comes along, her high heeled boots tapping on the pavement. She leads by the hand a curly—headed little girl who walks along waving two scarlet carnations in her hand and singing: "O, ma, O ma, O mia ma..."

Pausing behind the old navvy, the little girl stops singing, raises herself on her toes and looks gravely over his shoulder at the wine pouring into the yellow jug, with a gurgling sound like the continuation of her song.

She pulls her hand away from the woman's, quickly tears off the petals of her flowers and raising her little hand as dark as a sparrow's wing, she throws them into the wine jug.

The four men start and raise their dusty heads in anger. The little girl claps her hands and laughs and stamps her little feet. The embarrassed mother tries to catch her hand, scolding her in a high-pitched voice. The boy doubles up with laughter, and the petals of the flowers float on the dark wine in the jug like tiny pink boats.

The old man takes a glass, skims off the flowers along with the wine, rises and, putting the glass to his lips, says in a grave soothing voice:

"That's all right, signora: A child's gift is god's gift... Your health, fair signora, and yours too, child! May you be as beautiful as your mother and twice as happy."

He dips the ends of his grey moustache into the glass, screws up his eyes and slowly sips the wine, smacking his lips loudly and twitching his crooked nose.

The mother smiles, bows and moves on, leading the little girl by the hand, and the child shuffles her little feet over the pavement, swaying from side to side and singing:

"O, maa... O mia, ma..."

The navvies turn their heads lazily and with their eyes now on their wine, now on the little girl, and smile and say something to each other in their rapid southern dialect.

And in the jug the scarlet petals of the flowers still float on the surface of the crimson wine.

The sea sings, the city hums, the sun shines brightly, weaving its tales of magic.

THE TUNNEL

THE CALM BLUE lake is set in a frame of tall mountains crested by eternal snows. The dark tracery of gardens undulates in luxurious folds down to the water's edge. White houses that seem built of sugar gaze into the water and the stillness is like the gentle slumber of a child.

It is morning. The scent of flowers is wafted sweetly from the hills. The sun has just risen, and the dew-drops still glisten on the leaves of the trees and the blades of grass. The road is a grey ribbon flung into the silent mountain gorge, the road is paved with stones, yet it seems as if it must be soft as velvet to the touch.

Beside a heap of rubble sits a worker, as black as a beetle; his face expresses courage and kindliness and he wears a medal on his chest.

Resting his bronzed hands on his knees, he looks up into the face of the passer-by who stands under a chestnut tree.

"This medal, signor," he says, "is for my work on the Simplon tunnel."

And looking down, he smiles gently at the shining piece of metal on his chest.

"Yes, all work is hard until it gets into your bones and you learn to love it, and then it stirs you and ceases to be hard. But, of course, it wasn't easy!"

He shook his head slightly, smiling at the sun; then, livening up suddenly, he waved his hand and his black eyes glistened.

"Sometimes it was a bit frightening. Even the earth must feel something, don't you think? When we burrowed in deep, cutting a great gash into the mountainside, the earth inside there met us in anger. Its breath was hot, and our hearts sank, our heads grew heavy and our bones ached. Many have experienced the same thing! Then it hurled stones at us and doused us with hot water. That was awful! Sometimes when the light struck it, the water would turn red, and my father would say that we had wounded the earth and that it would drown and scorch us all with its blood! That was sheer imagination, of course, but when you hear such talk deep down inside the earth, in the suffocating darkness with the water dripping mournfully and the iron grating against the stone, everything seems possible. It was all so fantastic there, signor. We men seemed so puny compared with that mountain reaching up to the clouds, the mountain into whose bowels we were drilling... you would understand what I mean if you had seen it, seen the yawning gap we little men had made in the mountainside, seen us entering through that gap at dawn and the sun looking sadly after us as we burrowed into the earth's bowels; seen the machines, the gloomy face of the mountain, heard the heavy rumble deep within and the echo of the explosions sounding like the laughter of a madman."

He examined his hands, straightened the metal tab on his blue overall and sighed faintly.

"Men know how to work!" he continued with pride. "Ah, signor, man, small as he is, can be an invincible force when he wants to work. And, believe me, man puny as he is can do anything he sets out to do. My father didn't believe that at first.

" 'To cut through a mountain from one country to another,' he used to say, 'is defying God who divided land by walls of mountains. You'll see, the Madonna will forsake us!' He was mistaken, the Madonna never forsakes men who love her. Later on father came to think almost as I did, because he felt bigger and stronger than the mountain, but there was a time when he would sit at table on feast days with a bottle of wine in front of him and lecture me and the others.

" 'Children of God,' that was one of his favourite expressions, for he was a good, God-fearing man, 'children of God,' he would say, 'you can't fight the earth that way, she will take revenge for her wounds and will remain unvanquished! You will see: we shall bore our way right to the hearth of the mountain and when we touch it, we shall be hurled into the flames, because the heart of the earth is fire, everyone knows that! To till the earth is one thing, to help Nature with her birth pangs is man's duty, but to disfigure her face or her form—that we dare not to. See, the farther we bore into the mountain, the hotter becomes the air and the harder it is to breathe...' "

The man laughed softly, twirling his moustaches with his fingers.

"He wasn't the only one who thought thus, and indeed it was true: the farther we advanced, the hotter it grew, and more and more of us took ill and died. The hot springs gushed in ever more powerful streams, chunks of earth tore loose, and two of our men from

Lugano went insane. At night in the barracks many would rave in delirium, groan and leap from their beds in a fit of horror...

" 'Was I not right?' father said. There was terror in his eyes and his cough grew worse and worse... 'Was I not right?' he said. 'You can't defeat Nature!'

"And finally he took to his bed never to rise again. He was a sturdy old man, my father, and he battled with death for more than three weeks, stubbornly, uncomplainingly, like a man who knows his worth.

" 'My work is done, Paolo,' he said to me one night. 'Take care of yourself and go home, and may the Madonna be with you!' Then he was silent for a long time, and lay there breathing heavily with his eyes closed."

The man rose to his feet, glanced up at the mountains and stretched himself so that his sinews cracked.

"Then he took me by the hand and drew me close to him and said—God's truth, signor!—'Do you know, Paolo, my son, I think that it will be done just the same: We and those who are boring from the other side will meet within the mountain, we shall meet, you believe that, don't you, Paolo?' Yes, I believed it. 'That is well my son! A man must always believe in what he is doing, he must be confident of success and have faith in God who, thanks to the Madonna's prayers, helps good works. I beseech you, son, if it should happen, if the men meet inside the mountain, come to my grave and say: Father it is done! Then I shall know!'

"It was good, signor, and I promised him. He died five days later. Two days before his death he asked me and the others to bury him on the spot where he had worked inside the tunnel, he begged us to do it, but I think he must have been raving.

"We and those others who were moving toward us from the other side met in the mountain thirteen weeks after my father's death. Oh, that was a mad day, signor, that day when down there in the dark underground, we heard the first sounds of that other work, the sounds made by those coming to meet us in the bowels of the earth, signor, beneath the tremendous weight of earth that could have crushed us little men, all of us with one blow!

"For many days we heard these sounds, hollow sounds that grew louder and more distinct from day to day, and the wild joy of victors possessed us, we worked like fiends, like evil spirits, and felt no weariness, needed no urging. Ah, it was good, like dancing on a sunny day, it was, I swear to you! And we all became as kind and gentle as children. Ah, if you but knew how powerful, how passionate is the desire to meet other men in the darkness underground where you have been burrowing like a mole for many long months!"

His face flushed with excitement at the recollection. He came closer and gazing deeply with his profoundly human eyes into those of his listener, he continued in a soft, happy voice:

"And when finally the last intervening layer of earth crumbled and the bright yellow flame of the torch lit up the opening and we saw a black face streaming with tears of joy and more torches and faces behind it, shouts of victory thundered, shouts of joy—oh, that was the happiest day of my life, and when I recall it I feel that my life has not been in vain! That was work, my work, holy work, signor, I tell you! And when we emerged into the sunlight many of us fell to the ground and pressed our lips to it, weeping; it was as wonderful as a fairy tale! Yes, we kissed the vanquished mountain, kissed the earth; and that day I felt closer to the earth than I had ever been, signor, I loved it as one loves a woman!

"Of course, I went to my father's grave. I know that the dead cannot hear anything, but I went just the same, for one must respect the wishes of those who laboured for us and who suffered no less than we did, is that not so?

"Yes, yes, I went to his grave, knocked at the earth with my foot and said as he had bade me:

" 'Father, it is done!' I said. 'We men have conquered. It is done, father!' "

THE CITY

THE YOUNG MUSICIAN spoke softly, his dark eyes gazing into the distance. "This is what I would like to express in music," he said.

"A boy is walking along a road leading to a big city. It lies before him, a sombre mass of sprawling stone, clinging to the earth, groaning and muttering. From the distance it seems to have been destroyed by fire, for the lurid flame of the sunset still rises above it and the crosses of its churches, its spires and weather-vanes have an incandescent glow.

"The edges of the black clouds too seem on fire,

angular sections of huge buildings are outlined starkly against the red patches of sky, and here and there window—panes glitter like gaping wounds. The wrecked and anguished city, scene of a ceaseless struggle for happiness, seems to be bleeding to death and a hot yellowish suffocating smoke rises from it.

"The boy walks in the twilight a long the grey strip of road which thrusts itself straight as a sword into the side of the city, unerringly directed by some mighty invisible hand. The trees on either side of the road stand like unlighted torches, their large black limbs motionless over the silent expectant earth.

"The sky is covered with clouds, no stars are visible and there are no shadows. The late evening is melancholy and still, only the slow, light steps of the boy are faintly audible in the weary silence of the slumbering fields.

"Night advances noiselessly in the boy's wake, hiding with the dark mantle of oblivion the far distances from which he came.

"The gathering dusk enfolds in its warm embrace the solitary white and red houses that cling submissively to the earth, the gardens, the trees, the chimneys scattered desolately over the hills. The world turns black and disappears, crushed by the darkness of the night, as if hiding in fear from the small figure with the staff in its hand, or playing hide-and-seek with it.

"He walks on in silence, at the same unhurried pace, a small, lone figure, his eyes fixed steadily on the city ahead, as if he were the bearer of something momentous and long-awaited by those in the city, where blue, yellow and red lights are already twinkling a welcome to him.

"The sun has set. The crosses, weather-vanes and steeples have melted and disappeared. The city now seems shrunk and diminished, more densely packed against the silent earth.

"An opal cloud has appeared over it, a phosphorescent, yellowish mist hangs over the grey network of huddled buildings. The city no longer seems to have been destroyed by fire and drenched with blood; there is now something both mysterious and incomplete about the uneven line of its roofs and walls, as though he who started to build this great city for men to live in had grown weary and retired to rest, or perhaps, disappointed in what he had begun, had abandoned it and gone away or lost faith and died.

"But the city lives; it is possessed with an agonizing desire to see itself towering in proud beauty to the sun. It groans in a delirium of desire for happiness, it is a stir with a passionate will to live, and in the dark silence of the fields around it flow gentle streams of muffled sound, while the black bowl of the sky fills up more and more with a dim and dismal light.

"The boy stops, throws back his head and, peering into the distance with his serene courageous gaze, he quickens his pace.

"And the night, following on his heels, murmurs in the tender voice of a mother:

"'Tis time, child. Go! They are waiting for you!'

... "But of course it is impossible to write such music," the young musician said at length with a pensive smile.

Then clasping his hands together he exclaimed in tenderness and distress:

"Holy Mother of God! What will he find there?"

MIDDAY

THE SUN MELTS in the blue midday sky, pouring its hot rainbow-hued rays on to sea and earth. The drowsy sea exhales an opalescent mist, the blue water gleams like steel, and a strong scent of brine is wafted ashore.

The waves plash lazily against the grey boulders, spill over their backs and on to the whispering pebbles; they are small waves, as transparent as glass and untouched by foam.

A purple haze enwraps the mountain, the grey olive leaves are like old silver in the sunlight, the dark velvety green of the gardens terracing the hills is lit up by the golden glow of lemons and oranges, the scarlet pomegranate blossoms smile their vivid smile and there are flowers, flowers everywhere.

The sun truly loves this earth.

Two fishermen are on the rocky shore. One is an old man in a straw hat, with a round face and a grey stubble on his cheeks and chin, eyes half hidden in fat, a red nose and hands bronzed by the sun. Holding his slender fishing-rod far out over the water, he sits on a rock, his hairy legs dangling and the green waves leap up and lick his feet and heavy bright drops of water fall off his dark toes into the sea.

Behind the old man, leaning his elbow on a boulder, stands a dark-eyed, swarthy-skinned young man, tall and slender, with a red cap on his head, a white jersey stretched over his powerful chest, and blue trousers tucked up to the knees. He twirls his moustache and stares thoughtfully out to the sea to where the black strips of fishing boats are bobbing gently on the water, and in the far distance a motionless white sail, like a fluffy cloud melting in the heat, is faintly visible.

"Is she rich, the signora?" the old man asks in a hoarse voice, pulling in his line.

"I believe so," the young man replies softly. "She wore a brooch with a big blue stone, ear-rings and a great many rings and a watch. An American, I think."

"And is she beautiful?"

"Oh yes! Very slender, it is true, but eyes like flowers and a tiny slightly open mouth..."

"That is the mouth of an honest woman and one who loves but once in her life."

"That is what I think."

The old man swung up his rod, looked at the empty hook through narrowed eyes, grunted and remarked with a chuckle:

"Fish are no more foolish than we."

"Who goes fishing at midday?" said the young man, dropping on to his haunches.

"I do," said the old man and he baited his hook. Throwing the line far out into the sea, he asked:

You rowed till morning, you say?"

"Yes, the sun was already rising when we came ashore," replied the young one with a deep sigh.

"Twenty lire?"

"Yes."

"She could have given more."

"She could have given much..."

"What did you two talk about?"

The young man's head drooped sadly.

"She knows no more than ten words of Italian, and so we were silent..."

"True love," said the old man, turning to him and

showing his white teeth in a broad smile, "strikes the heart like lightning and is as silent as lightning, too, surely you know that?"

Picking up a big stone, the young man was about to throw it out into the sea, but changed his mind and threw it over his shoulder instead.

"Sometimes," he said, "you wonder why people need so many different languages."

"They say that one day it will not be so," remarked the old man after a pause.

A white steamer, like the shadow of a cloud, slid noiselessly in the milky haze at the far edge of the sea's expanse.

"Bound for Sicily," said the old man, nodding in its direction.

He produced a long, rough, black cigar from somewhere, broke it in two and handed the young man a half over his shoulder.

"What were you thinking of when you sat with her in that boat?"

"A man always thinks of happiness..."

"That is why he is always a fool," observed the old man.

They lighted up. The blue spirals of smoke curled over the stones in the still air which was saturated with the satisfying smell of the fecund earth and the gentle water.

"I sang to her and she smiled to me..."

"And what then?"

"Well, you know I am not much of a singer."

"No."

"So I rested the oars and gazed at her."

"You did?"

"I gazed at her and thought to myself—here am I, young and strong, and you are bored. Love me and let me live a good life."

"Is she bored?"

"Who will travel to a strange land if he is not poor and if he is happy?"

"Bravo!"

"I vow to you by the Virgin Mary," I thought to myself, "that I shall be good to you and everyone will be happy around us..."

"Ecco!" exclaimed the old man, and he threw back his big head and laughed heartily.

"I shall be true to you always..."

"Hm..."

"Or, I thought, we shall live together for a while and I shall love you as much as you wish, and then you will give me money to buy a boat and tackle and a plot of land and I shall return to my own country and remember you with gratitude all my life."

"That is not foolish..."

"Then toward morning, I thought that perhaps I did not want anything. I did not want money, I only wanted her, at least for that one night."

"That is simpler."

"For only one night!"

"Ecco!" said the old man.

"It seems to me, Uncle Petro, that a little happiness is always more honest..."

The old man said nothing. He pursed his thick lips and stared out at the green water, while the young man began to sing on a soft sad note:

"O sole mio..."

"Yes, yes," the old man said suddenly, shaking his head. "A little happiness is more honest, but much happiness is better still. Poor men are handsomer, the rich are more powerful. And thus it is in all things!"

The waves continued their ceaseless murmur. Blue wisps of smoke floated over the heads of the men like haloes. The young man rose to his feet, humming a tune with the cigar in a corner of his mouth. He stood with his shoulder leaning against a grey boulder, his arms folded over his chest, gazing out to sea with a dreamy look in his eyes.

And the old man sat motionless, his head lowered. He seemed to be dozing.

The purple shadows in the mountains thickened and grew softer.

"O sole mio!" sang the young man.

> The sun was born
> More beautyful,
> More beautyful than thou.
> Oh, sun,
> Shine in my breast!

The green waves kept up their gay frolic.

THE WEDDING

At a small station between Rome and Genoa the conductor opened the door of our compartment and with the aid of a grimy oiler almost carried in a little old man blind in one eye.

"Very old!" they chorussed, smiling good-naturedly.

But the old man turned out to be quite spry. Thanking his assistants with a wave of his wrinkled hand, he raised his battered hat from his hoary head with gay politeness and, glancing at the benches with his keen eye, inquired:

"Permit me?"

The passengers moved up and he sat down with a sigh of relief, resting his hands on his bony knees, his lips parted in a good-natured toothless smile.

"Travelling far, Grandpa?" my companion asked him.

"Oh no, only three stations from here!" was the old one's ready reply. "I'm going to my grandson's wedding..."

A few minutes later to the accompaniment of the rhythmic beat of the wheels he was telling us his story, swaying from side to side like a broken branch on a stormy day.

"I'm a Ligurian," he said. "We, Ligurians, are a sturdy lot. Take me, I've got thirteen sons and four daughters and I don't know how many grandchildren. This is the second to get married. Pretty good, eh?"

And proudly surveying us all with his single eye, dimmed yet merry still, he chuckled.

"See how many people I've given my king and country!"

"How did I lose my eye? Ah, that happened a long time ago. I was just a bit of a lad then, but I was already helping my father. He was turning the soil in the vineyard—the soil down our way is hard and stony and needs a deal of attention—when a stone flew up from under his pickaxe and hit me right in the eye.

I don't remember feeling any pain, but that day while I was eating my dinner my eye fell out. That was awful, signori! They stuck it back and put a warm bread poultice on but it was no use, the eye was gone!"

The old man vigorously rubbed his sallow flabby cheek and again smiled his jolly, good-humoured smile.

"In those days there weren't as many doctors as there are now and people lived foolishly. Oh, yes! But perhaps they were kinder, eh?"

Now his one-eyed, leathery face, deeply lined and overgrown with greenish-grey hair like mould, assumed a look of sly triumph.

"When a man has lived as long as I have, he can say what he thinks of people, don't you think so?"

He raised a dark, crooked finger gravely as though reproving someone.

"Let me tell you something about people, signori..."

"I was thirteen when my father died, and was smaller even than I am now. But I was a spry lad and tireless when it came to work. That was all I inherited from my father, for our plot of land and the house were sold to cover our debts. And so I lived with my one eye and my two hands, working wherever there was work to be found... It was hard, but youth is not afraid of hardships, is it?

"When I was nineteen I meet the girl whom I was

fated to love. She was as poor as I was, but she was a strapping lass and stronger than me. She lived with her old invalid mother and like myself did whatever work came her way. She wasn't especially handsome but she was kind and had a good head on her shoulders. And a fine voice, too. Ah, how she could sing! Just like a professional. And a good voice is worth a great deal. I used to sing quite well myself.

"'Shall we get married?' I asked her one day.

"'That would be foolish, one-eyed one!' she replied sadly. 'Neither your nor I have anything. How should we live?'

"That was God's truth: neither of us owned anything. But what does a young couple in love need? You know yourselves how little love requires. I insisted and won my point.

"'Well, perhaps you're right,' said my Ida at last. 'If the Holy Mother helps us now, when we live apart how much easier will it be for her to help us when we live together!'

"And so we went to the priest.

"'This is madness!' he said. 'Are there not enough beggars in Liguria as it is? Unhappy people, you are the devil's playthings, resist his temptations or you will pay dearly for you weakness!'

"The young folk in the community laughed at us,

the old folk censured us. But youth is stubborn and wise in its own way! The wedding day arrived, we were no richer on that day than before and we did not even know where we would lay us down to sleep on our wedding night.

"'Let us go to the fields!' said Ida. 'Why not? The mother of God is kind to people wherever they may be.'

"And so we decided—let the earth be our bed and the sky our counterpane.

"And now begins another story, signori. I beg your attention, for this is the best story in all my long life!

"Early in the morning the day before our wedding, old Giovanni for whom I had done a good deal of work said to me, muttering under his breath because he disliked to speak of such trifles:

"'You ought to clean out the old sheep pen, Ugo. Put in some clean straw. It's dry and the sheep haven't been there for more than a year, but you'd best clean it out if you and Ida want to live in it.'

"And there was our house!

"As I was busy cleaning out the sheep pen, singing at my work, I looked up to see Costanzio, the carpenter, standing in the doorway.

"'So this is where you and Ida are going to live? But where is your bed? I have an extra one at my place. Come over and get it when you've finished cleaning.'

"As I was going to him, Maria, the shrewish shopkeeper, shouted:

"'Getting married, the fools, with not a sheet or a pillow to call their own! You are crazy, one-eyed one, but send your bride to me...'

"And lame Ettore Viano, for ever tortured by rheumatism and fever, cried out to her from his doorstep:

"'Ask him how much wine he has put by for the guests? Ah, how can people be so thoughtless!'"

A bright tear glistened in one of the deep folds on the old man's cheek, he threw back his head and laughed soundlessly, his bony Adam's apple working and his loose skin trembling.

"Oh, signori, signori," he said, choking with laughter and waving his hands in childish glee. "On the morning of our wedding day we had everything we needed for our home—a statue of the Madonna, dishes, linen, furniture, everything, I swear to you! Ida laughed and wept. I too, and everyone else laughed—for it is bad to weep on a wedding day, and all our own folks laughed at us!

"Signori! It is damned fine to have the right to call people your own. And even better to feel them your own kith and kin, people for whom your life is not a joke and your happiness a gamble!

"And what a wedding it was! What a day! The whole community attended the ceremony, and everyone came to our sheep pen which had all at once become a rich mansion... We had everything! Wine and fruit, meat and bread, and everyone ate and everyone was gay... That, signori, is because there is no greater happiness than to do good to people, believe me, there is nothing finer and more beautiful than that!

"And the priest came too. He made a fine speech. 'Here', he said, 'are two people who have worked for all of you, and you have done what you could to make this day the best in their lives. And that is as it should be, for they have worked for you, and work is more important than copper and silver money, work is always more important than the remuneration you receive for it! Money goes, but work remains... These people are gay and modest, their life has been hard yet they did not complain, their lives will be harder still and still they will not grumble, you will help them in their hour of need. They have good hands and stout hearts.'

"And he said many flattering things to me, to Ida and to the whole community!"

The old man surveyed us all with an eye that was young again:

"There, signori, I have told you something about people. It was good, was it not?"

THE PROPAGANDIST

It is spring the sun shines brightly, everyone is gay and even the windows of the old stone houses seem to be smiling.

A crowd of people dressed in their holiday clothes pours in a colourful stream through the streets of the little town. The whole town is here—workingmen, soldiers, burghers, priests, officials, fisherman—all slightly intoxicated by the spring, talking loudly, laughing and singing and all, like a single body, bursting with the joy of being alive.

The coloured parasols and hats of the women, the

read and blue balloons carried by the children all resemble fantastic flowers, and everywhere, glowing and scintillating like the precious gems on the sumptuous robes of a fairy-tale king, are the laughing children, the happy monarchs of the earth.

The pale green foliage of the trees is still folded into tight little buds which are greedily drinking in the warm rays of the sun. Music sounds invitingly in the distance.

One feels as if men's misfortunes are a thing of the past, as if yesterday had seen the end of the hard life they had so long endured, and today everyone had awakened feeling as light-hearted as children, conscious of a new-found confidence and faith in their indomitable will which must carry all before it, and were now marching confidently together toward the future.

And it was strange and sad to observe in this lively throng the sorrowful face of a tall, sturdily built man walking past with a young woman on his arm. He could have been hardly more than thirty, yet his hair was grey. He held his hat in his hand, exposing his round silvery head. His lean, healthy face wore a calm, yet sorrowful expression, and his large dark eyes half hidden by the lids were the eyes of one who has suffered pain that cannot be forgotten.

"Observe that couple," my friend said to me. "Especially the man. He is the victim of a tragedy that is becoming more and more common among the workers of Northern Italy."

And he proceeded to tell me this story.

That man is a Socialist, he said, the editor of a local workers' newspaper. He is a worker himself, a house painter by trade, one of those natures for whom knowledge is faith and faith increases the desire for knowledge. A passionate and intelligent anti-clerical. See the dark looks those black-robed priests cast in his direction!

Some five years ago he met a young girl in one of the study-circles he led as a propagandist. The women here have been taught to cherish a blind and unshakable belief in God, the priests have worked for centuries to imbue them with this capacity and they have achieved their purpose. Someone has said quite correctly that the Catholic Church has been built up on the breasts of women. The cult of the Madonna is not only beautiful in the pagan sense, it is a very clever cult. The Madonna is simpler than Christ, She is nearer to the heart, She is torn by no inner conflicts, She carries no threat of Gehenna, She is all love, compassion and forgiveness. It is easy for Her to take possession of a woman's heart for life.

But here was a young woman who was able to speak up and ask questions, and in her questions this man felt besides naïve wonder at his ideas, an undisguised distrust of him, mingled often with fear and even revulsion. The Italian propagandist is obliged to speak much about religion, and often to speak in harsh terms of the Pope and the clergy. And each time he spoke of this he read in the girl's eyes scorn and hatred for himself, and if she asked him a question her words had a hostile ring, and there was poison in her gentle voice. She was clearly conversant with Catholic literature directed against socialism and in this study-circle her words were obviously listened to with no less interest than his own.

Here in Italy the attitude to women is much cruder than in Russia, and until quite recently Italian women themselves were largely to blame for this. Taking no interest in anything besides the Church, they are at best indifferent to the cultural activity of their menfolk and do not understand its significance.

Our friend's masculine pride was hurt, his fame as a skilled propagandist suffered in his clashes with this young girl. He sometimes lost his temper, and several times cleverly ridiculed her argument, but she repaid him in kind, arousing his reluctant respect and compelling him to take particular care in preparing for his lecture to the class she attended.

Yet at the same time he noticed that whenever he spoke of the ugliness of contemporary life, how it oppressed man, how it crippled his body and soul, and whenever he painted pictures of life in the future when man would be free morally and physically, a remarkable change would come over his antagonist. She listened to him with the wrath of a strong and intelligent woman who knew how heavy life's chains could be, and with the trustful eagerness of a child listening to some wondrous fairy—tale that is in harmony with its own enchanted soul.

This aroused in him the hope of ultimately winning over an opponent who might prove to be a fine comrade.

For nearly a year the contest lasted without evoking in either of them any desire to become more closely acquainted and to carry on their debate eye to eye. But at last he approached her.

"Signorina is my constant antagonist," he said. "Does she not think that in the interests of the cause it would be well for us to get to know each other better?"

She willingly agreed and almost at once they crossed swords: she hotly defending the Church as a place where the tortured soul of man could find peace, where all were equal before the good Madonna, all objects alike of compassion whatever their garb; he objecting that it was not rest man needed, but struggle, that social equality was impossible without equality of material benefits, and that behind the Madonna lurked men to whose advantage it was to keep people unhappy and ignorant.

Thenceforward these debates filled their entire lives. Each encounter was a continuation of one and the same passionate argument, and with each succeeding day the utter irreconcilability of their beliefs became more and more apparent.

For him life meant a striving for knowledge, a struggle to subordinate the mysterious forces of nature to the human will. All men, he argued, must be equally armed for that struggle which must culminate in freedom and the triumph of reason—the mightiest of all forces and the only force in the world that operates consciously. For her, life was an agonizing sacrifice to the unknown, a subordination of the mind to a will, a law and a goal known to the priest alone.

"Then why do you come to my lectures?" he demanded in amazement. "What do you expect of socialism?"

"Ah, I know that it is sinful of me, that I am going against my better judgement," she admitted sorrowfully. "But it is so good to listen to you and to dream of the possibility of happiness for all men on earth!"

She was not especially beautiful—a slender girl, with an intelligent face and large eyes whose expression could be mild and wrathful, tender and stern. She worked at a silk mill, and lived with her aged mother, a crippled father and a younger sister who attended a trade school. Sometimes she was gay, not noisily merry, but charmingly gay. She adored museums and old churches, she took delight in paintings and in beautiful objects, and gazing at them she would say:

"How strange it is to think that these beautiful things were once locked up in the homes of private persons and that one person only had the right to enjoy them! Beauty must be accessible to all, only then does it truly live!"

She often spoke so strangely that it seemed to him that her words sprang from some secret agony of soul, for they reminded him of the groans of a wounded man. He felt that this girl loved life and people with the deep love of a mother, a love full of anxiety and compassion. He waited patiently for the moment when his faith would touch off the spark in her heart that would turn her gentle love to passion. It seemed to him that she listened more and more eagerly to his talks, and that in her heart she already agreed with him. And with greater fervour than ever he spoke to her of the need for incessant struggle for the liberation of mankind from the old fetters whose rust was eating into the soul of men and poisoning them.

One day as he escorted her to her home he told her that he loved her and wished to marry her. He was shocked by the effect his declaration had upon her. She recoiled as if he had struck her. Her eyes opened wide and she leaned, pale-faced, against the wall for support, her hands hidden behind her back.

"I guessed it," she said, gazing at him with something like horror. "I felt it, because I too have loved you for a long time. But, Oh my God, what shall we do?"

"We shall be happy, you and I together, we shall work side by side!" he exclaimed.

"No," said the girl, and her head drooped. "No! There can be no talk of love between us two."

"Why?"

"Will you marry me in Church?" she asked in a low voice.

"No!"

"Then, farewell!"

And she walked swiftly away from him.

He caught up with her and began to plead with her. She listened to him in silence, then she said:

"I, my mother and my father are all religious and we shall die religious. Marriage by magistrate is not for me. Children who are born of such a marriage are bound to be unfortunate, I know it. Church marriage alone sanctifies love, it alone can give happiness and peace."

He saw that she would not easily give in, but neither could he yield on that point. They parted. As she took leave of him, the girl said:

"Let us not torment each other. Do not try to see me any more. Ah, if only you would go away from here. I cannot, I am too poor..."

"I can give you no promises," he replied.

Thus began the struggle between these two strong people. They met, of course, and even more frequently than before. They met because they wanted to meet, each hoping that the other would be unable to withstand the torture of unrequited passion that burned ever more intensely. Their meetings were full of anguish and despair. Each time he felt crushed and helpless, while she went away weeping to confession, and he knew it and it seemed to him that the black wall of men with tonsured heads grew higher and more formidable from day to day, threatening to part them for ever.

Once, on some holiday, as they were walking

together in a meadow in the country, he said to her:

"Sometimes it seems to me that I could kill you." It was not a threat, he was merely thinking aloud.

She did not reply.

"Did you hear what I said?"

"Yes," she replied, glancing up tenderly at him.

And he realized that she would die before she gave in to him. Before that "yes" he had sometimes embraced her and kissed her. She had struggled a little, but her resistance had grown weaker and he had begun to hope that one day she would yield to him and that her womanly instinct would help him to conquer her. But now he knew that this would be not victory but enslavement, and thenceforth he ceased trying to awaken the woman in her.

Thus he explored with her the dark confines of her narrow conception of life. He sought to flood that darkness with the light of knowledge, but she listened to him like a blind creature with a dreamy smile on her lips and disbelief in her heart.

"Sometimes I realize that everything you tell me is indeed possible," she said once. "But then I think that is because I love you. I understand, but I do not believe, I cannot believe! And when you leave me everything that is yours goes with you."

This lasted for nearly two years, and one day the girl fell ill. He gave up his work, abandoned his political activity, got into debt and, avoiding his comrades, spent his time outside her apartment or at her bedside watching her consumed with fever, seeing her wasting away with each passing day as the flames of sickness leapt higher and higher.

"Tell me about the future," she begged him.

But he spoke to her of the present, fiercely enumerating all that which is destroying us, which he would always fight against and which must be cast out of the lives of men like so many filthy, worn-out rags.

She listened, and when the pain became unendurable she stopped him, touching his hand and gazing imploringly into his eyes.

"Am I dying?" she asked him once, many days after the doctor had told him that she had galloping consumption and that her condition was hopeless.

He turned away.

"I know that I will die soon," she said. "Give me your hand."

And when he stretched his hand out to her she pressed her hot lips to it.

"Forgive me," she said. "I have wronged you, I

71

ought not to have tormented you. I see now that my faith was nothing but fear of that which I could not understand in spite of my own desire and your efforts. It was fear, but that fear is in my blood. I was born with it. I have my own mind—or perhaps yours—but my heart does not belong to me. You are right, I knew it, but my heart could not agree with you."

A few days later she was dead, and as he watched her death agony his hair turned grey. Grey at twenty-seven.

Not long ago he married that girl's only friend, also a pupil of his. They are on their way now to the cemetery. They go there every Sunday to put flowers on her grave.

He does not believe in his victory. He is convinced that when she told him that he was right, she was lying in order to console him. His wife thinks the same, both of them cherish her memory, and her tragic story inspires them to avenge the death of a splendid human being, lends boundless energy and a peculiar beauty to their joint efforts...

...The gay, colourful throng of people flows like a bright river under the sun, the sound of merriment accompanies its course, children shout and laugh as they go. True, not everyone is light-hearted and gay, doubtless many hearts are heavy with sorrow, many minds tortured by doubt, but we are all marching forward to liberty, to liberty!

And the closer we march together, the faster our progress!

THE MOTHER

Lᴇᴛ ᴜs ʀᴀɪsᴇ our voices in praise of woman, the Mother, inexhaustible fount of all-conquering life!

This is the tale of the flint-hearted Timur-i-leng, the lame panther, of Sakhib-i-Kirani, the lucky conqueror, of Tamerlane, as he was called by the infidels, of the man who sought to destroy the whole world.

For fifty years he trampled the earth, his iron heel crushing cities and states as the foot of an elephant crushes an ant-hill. Red rivers of blood flowed in his wake in all directions. He built tall towers out of the bones of vanquished peoples. He destroyed life, pitting his power against the power of Death, for he was avenging the death of his son Jigangir. A ghastly man, he wished to rob Death of all his

75

spoils so that he might expire from hunger and despair!

From the day when his son Jigangir died and the people of Samarkand met the conqueror of the evil Juts dressed in black and pale-blue, their heads sprinkled with dust and ashes, from that day until the hour in Otrav thirty years later when Death overpowered him at last, Timur did not smile. He lived thus with lips compressed, his head unbowed and his heart locked against compassion—for thirty years!

Let us sing the praises of woman, the Mother, the sole force before which Death humbly bows his head! Let here be told the truth about Mother, how Death's servant and slave, the stony-hearted Tamerlane, the bloody scourge of the earth, bowed before her.

It came about thus: in the lovely valley of Canigula wreathed in clouds of roses and jasmine, the valley Samarkand poets named "Vale of Flowers," whence the blue minarets of the great city, the blue cupolas of the mosques are visible, Timur-bek was feasting.

Fifteen thousand circular tents were spread out fanwise in the valley like fifteen thousand tulips, and over each tent hundreds of silken pennants fluttered in the breeze.

And in the centre stood the tent of Gurugan Timur, like a queen among her train. It was four-cornered, each side one hundred paces in length, three spears in height, the centre was supported by twelve golden columns each as thick as a man; atop rested a pale-blue cupola while the sides were of black, yellow and blue striped silk; five hundred scarlet cords kept it fixed firmly to the ground so that it might not rise into the sky, four silver eagles stood at its corners, and under the cupola on a dais in the centre of the tent sat the fifth eagle, the king of kings himself, the invincible Timur-Gurugan.

He was garbed in a flowing silken robe of a celestial hue studded with pearls, five thousand large pearls no less. On his fearsome grey head sat a white peaked cap with a ruby on the tip that swayed to and fro like a bloodshot eye surveying the world.

The face of the Lame One was like a broad-bladed knife, rusty from the blood into which it had been immersed thousands of times; his eyes were narrow slits that missed nothing, and their glitter was the cold glitter of the zaramut, favourite gem of the Arabs which the infidels call emerald and which cures the falling sickness. And from his ears suspended ear-rings of Ceylon rubies, the colour of a lovely maiden's lips.

On the floor of the tent on carpets of unsurpassed beauty stood three hundred golden jugs of wine and everything meet for a kingly feast; behind Timur sat the musicians, beside him no one, and at his feet, his kinsmen, kings and princes and chieftains, and closest to him of all drunken Kermani, the poet, who, when the destroyer of the world once asked him:

"Kermani! How much wouldst thou give for me, were I to be sold?" had replied: "Twenty-five askers."

"But my belt alone is worth as much!" Timur had exclaimed in amazement.

"It is of thy belt that I was thinking," replied Kirmani, "only of thy belt, for thou thyself art not worth a farthing!"

So spake Kermani, the poet, to the king of kings, the man of horror and evil, and may the glory of the poet, friend of truth, be ever exalted above the glory of Tamerlane!

Let us sing the praises of poets who know but one God, the fearless, beautiful word of truth. That is their God for ever!

And so in the hour when the revelry and feasting, the proud reminiscences of battles and victories, were at their height, in the midst of the loud music and the popular games played in front of the king's tent, where innumerable piebald jesters bounded up and down, where athletes wrestled and tight-rope walkers went through such contortions that one would think there was not a bone in their bodies, and warriors

78

crossed swords exhibiting peerless skill in the art of killing, and performances were given with elephants painted red and green which made some appear frightful and others ridiculous—at that hour of rejoicing among Timur's men, who were intoxicated with fear of him, with pride in his glory, with weariness of victories, with wine and koumiss—at that wild hour the cry of a woman, the proud cry of a she-eagle reached the ears of Sultan Bayezid's conqueror, suddenly cutting through the hubbub, like a streak of lightning through a thundercloud. It was a sound familiar to him and in harmony with his wounded soul, the soul wounded by Death and hence cruel toward living men.

He ordered his men to see who it was that had cried out in joyless voice, and he was told that a woman, a mad creature in dust and rags, had come speaking in the language of the Arabs and demanding, yes demanding, to see him, the ruler of three cardinal points of the earth.

"Bring her in!" said the king.

And so before him stood a woman. She was barefoot and her tattered clothing had faded in the sun, her black tresses were loosened so that they covered her bare breast, her face was the colour of bronze and her eyes imperious, and her dark hand outstretched toward the Lame One did not tremble.

79

"Is it thou hast vanquished Sultan Bayezid?" she demanded.

"Yes, I have defeated him and many besides, and am not yet weary of conquests. And what saith thou of thyself, woman?"

"Hear me!" said she. "Whatever thou hast done, thou art but a man. I am a Mother! Thou servest death, I serve life. Thou hast sinned against me and so I have come to demand that thou atone for thy guilt. I have been told that thy device is 'in justice lies strength,' I do not believe it, but to me thou must be just, for I am a Mother!"

The king had wisdom enough to feel the power behind these bold words.

"Sit down and speak. I would listen to thee!"

She seated herself upon the carpet amid the intimate circle of kings and began her tale:

"I am from the region of Salerno, far away in Italy, thou knowest not those parts! My father was a fisherman, my husband too, he was as handsome as only happy men are and it was I who gave him happiness! I had a son too, the loveliest child in the world..."

"Like my Jigangir," the old warrior murmured.

"There is none as handsome and as clever a lad as my son! He was six years old when the Saracen pirates landed on our coast. They slew my father and my husband and many others, and they carried off my boy and for four years now I have been searching the earth for him. Now thou hast him. This I know, for Bayezid's men captured the pirates, and thou hast conquered Bayezid and taken all his possessions. Thou must know where my son is and give him back to me!"

Everyone laughed and the kings, who always consider themselves to be wise, said:

"She is made!" said the kings and the friends of Timur, the princes and chieftains, and they laughed.

Only Kermani gazed at the woman gravely and Tamerlane looked at her in great wonder.

"She is mad as a Mother is mad," the drunken poet Kermani said softly; and the king, the enemy of peace, said:

"Woman! How hast thou come hither from that unknown land acroos the seas, the rivers and mountains, through woods and forests? How is it that beasts and men—often more savage than the most savage of beasts—have not molested thee, how couldst thou have wandered alone without a weapon, which is the only friend of the defenceless and which will not betray him so long as he has strength to wield it? I must know this in order that I might believe thee and that my wonder might not prevent me from understanding what thou sayest!"

Let us sing the praises of woman, the Mother, whose love knows no obstacles, whose breast has nurtured the whole world! All that is beautiful in man, is derived from the sun's rays and from his Mother's milk. This it is that imbues us with love of life!

"I encountered but one sea in my wanderings," she replied. "There were many islands and fishing boats on it, and when one seeks a loved one the winds are always fair. And for one who has been born and brought up on the seashore it is no hardship to swim rivers. Mountains? I did not notice them."

And the drunken Kermani said gaily:

"A mountain becomes a valley for one who loves!"

"There were forests, yes. I encountered wild boars, bears, lynxes and fearful bulls with their heads bent low and twice panthers looked at me with eyes like thine own. But every animal has a heart, and I spoke with them as I speak with thee, they believed me when I said I was a Mother, and they went their way sighing, for they pitied me! Knowest thou not that the beasts too love their children and know how to fight for their lives and freedom no less than men?"

"Well said, woman," said Timur. "And often, this I know, they love more strongly and fight more stubbornly than men!"

"Men," she continued, like a child, for every Mother

82

is a child a hundredfold at heart, "men are always children to their mothers, for every man has a Mother, every man is some mother's son, even thou, old man, wast born of woman, thou canst deny God, but this thou canst never deny!"

"Well said, woman!" exclaimed Kermani, the fearless poet. "Well said! From a herd of bullocks there will be no calves, without the sun flowers will not bloom, without love there is no happiness, without woman there is no love, without Mothers there are neither poets nor heroes!"

And the woman said:

"Give me back my child, for I am his Mother and I love him."

Let us bow to Woman; she gave birth to Moses, to Mohammed and to Jesus, the great prophet who was put to death by evil men but who, as Sharifu 'd-Din hath said, shall rise again and bring judgement upon the living and the dead, and this shall come to pass in Damascus, in Damascus!

Let us bow to Her who tirelessly gives birth to the great! Aristotle is Her son, and Firdusi, and Saadi, as sweet as honey, and Omar Khayyam, like unto wine mixed with poison, Iskander and the blind Homer —these are all Her children, all of them imbibed her milk and She led each one of them into the world by the hand when they were no bigger than tulips. All the pride of the world comes from Mothers!

And the hoary destroyer of cities, the lame tiger Timur-Gurugan sat sunk in thought. After a long silence he said to those gathered about him:

"Men tangri Kuli Timur! I, God's servant Timur, do say what must be said! Thus I have lived, for many years the earth has groaned beneath my feet, and for thirty years I have been destroying it in order to avenge the death of my son Jigangir, for extinguishing the sun of life in my heart! Men have fought against me for kingdoms and cities, but never has anyone fought me for man, and never has man had any value in my sight, and I did not know who he was and why he stood in my path! It is I, Timur, who said to Bayezid when I defeated him: 'Oh, Bayezid, it must be that before God countries and men are nothing, for behold, he suffers them to be possessed by such as we: thou, one-eyed and I, lame!' So spake I to him when he was brought to me in chains and could barely stand under their weight, so spake I, gazing upon him in misfortune, and life at that moment was to me as bitter as wormwood, the weed of ruins!

"I, God's servant Timur, say what must be said! Here before me sits a woman, one of myriads, and she has awakened in my soul feelings such as I have never known. She speaks to me as to an equal, and she does not beg, she demands. And I see now, I understand why this woman is so strong—she loves, and love has taught her that her child is the spark of life which can kindle a flame for many centuries. Were not all the prophets children too, and were not all the heroes weak? O, Jigangir, light of mine eyes, perhaps thou wert destined to kindle the earth, to sow it with happiness, I, thy father, have drenched it with blood and it has grown fat!"

Once again the scourge of the nations lapsed into silence, then at last he spoke:

"I, God's servant Timur, say what must be said! Three hundred horsemen shall set out at once to all corners of my land and they shall find this woman's son and she shall wait here, and I shall wait with her; he who returns with the child in his saddle, good fortune shall be his—It is I, Timur, who speaks. Have I spoken well, woman?"

She tossed her black hair back from her face, smiled to him and replied:

"Thou hast, king!"

Then rose this terrible old man and in silence bowed to her, and the merry poet Kermani spake up with great rejoicing:

What is more beautiful than the song of flowers and stars?
The answer all men know: 'tis the song of love!
What is more beauteous than the sunlight at noon in May?
The lover replies: She whom I love!

Ah, beautiful are the stars in the midnight sky,
And beautiful the sun on a summer's noontide,
But the eyes of beloved are lovelier than all the flowers,
And her smile is more gentle than the sun's rays.

But the song most beautiful of all is yet to be sung,
The song of the beginning of all things on earth,
The song of the world's heart, of the magic heart,
Of her whom on earth we call Mother!

And Timur said to his poet:

"Good, Kermani! God was not mistaken when he chose thy lips to extol his wisdom!"

"God is himself a great poet!" spake the drunken Kermani.

And the woman smiled and all the kings smiled and the princes, and the chieftains smiled, they were all children as they gazed upon her—upon the Mother!

All this is true; every word spoken here is the truth, our mothers know it to be so, ask them and they will tell you:

"Yes, all this is the eternal truth, we are stronger than death, we who are for ever bringing into the world sages, poets and heroes, we who imbue man with all that makes him glorious!"

THE MONSTER

Iт is a нот day and all is hushed. The world is
silent and at peace. The blue orb od the sky looks
down tenderly upon the earth; the sun is its fiery
pupil.

The sea is a sheet of smooth blue metal. The varicoloured fishing boats stand motionless as if welded
into the semi-circle of the bay, as dazzlingly bright
as the sky. A sea-gull flies by, lazily flapping its wings,
and on the surface of the water another bird appears,
whiter and more beautiful than the one in the air.

In the shimmering distance a purple islet floats

gently on the water, or melts perhaps under the burning rays of the sun—a lone rock rising out of the sea, a bright gem in the diadem that is the Gulf of Naples.

The rocky coast descends in jagged ledges down to the sea; it is covered with a luxurious tangle of dark vines, orange-trees, lemons and figs, of pale silver olive leaves. Flowers, gold, red and white, smile gently through the dense foliage dropping steeply down to the sea, and the yellow and orange fruits remind one of stars on a warm moonlight night when the sky is dark and the air moist.

Sky, sea and soul are hushed, and in this stillness one yearns to hear the silent hymn life offers up to the Sun God.

A tall woman in black is walking down a path that winds between the gardens, stepping lightly from stone to stone. Her dress has faded in the sun to a splotchy brown, and even from the distance one can see the patches on the worn fabric. Her head is bare and her hair gleams silver, falling in tiny curls over her tall forehead, temples and her dark-skinned cheeks, the sort of hair that it is impossible to comb smooth.

Her face is sharp-featured and stern. It is a face which once seen can never be forgotten. There is something timeless in that stern face, and if you happen to meet the straight glance of her dark eyes you cannot help thinking of the burning deserts of the East, of Deborah and Judith.

She walks with head bent, crocheting as she goes. The steel of her crochet hook glitters, the ball of wool is hidden somewhere in her clothing, and it seems that the crimson thread seeps out of the woman's heart. The path is steep and wayward, now and again one hears the rattling of the stones as they drop down, but this grey-haired woman moves as confidently as if her feet had eyes to see the way.

Here is the tale they tell of this woman. She is a widow, her husband, a fisherman, went off on a fishing trip soon after they were married and never returned. She was left with a child under her heart.

When the child was born she hid it from people. She did not take it out into the street and the sunshine to show it off as all mothers do. She kept it in a dark corner of her hut swaddled in rags, and for a long time all that the neighbours saw of the infant was a large head and a pair of huge motionless eyes in a yellow face. It was observed too that this healthy, agile woman who had once fought poverty tirelessly and cheerfully imbuing others with energy and vigour, had now grown silent and downcast, looking at the world through a veil of sorrow, with a strange questioning look in her eyes.

It was not long before everyone learned her misfortune: her child was deformed, and that was why she had kept him hidden, this was the reason for her misery.

When they discovered this, the neighbours told her that they understood how shameful it was for a woman to give birth to a freak, that none but the Madonna knew whether this cruel fate was a just punishment, but however that might be, the child was not to blame and she was wrong to deprive it of sunlight.

She listened to them and showed them her son. They saw a monster with arms and legs as short as the fins of a fish, an enormous swollen head wobbling on a thin scraggy neck, a wrinkled old man's face, glazed eyes and a huge mouth spread into a deathly grin.

The women wept at the sight, the men looked at it with repugnance and turned away in silence. The mother of the monster sat on the ground, now hiding her face, now raising her head and staring at her neighbours with a wordless question none could understand.

The neighbours made a coffin-like box, filled it with the combings of wool and rags, placed the deformed creature in this soft warm nest and stood it in a shady part of the courtyard in the secret hope that the sun which worked wonders every day would perform another miracle.

But time went by and the enormous head, the long body with the four helpless limbs did not change. Only his smile began to acquire a definite expression of insatiable greed, and the mouth became filled with two rows of sharp crooked teeth. The foreshortened paws learned to seize pieces of bread and direct them almost unerringly into the large, hot mouth.

He was mute, but whenever the odours of food reached him, he would utter whining noises, open his maw and shake his heavy head, and the murky whites of his eyes would turn bloodshot.

He ate vastly, his capacity for food increased as time went on, and his whining was constant. His mother toiled ceaselessly, but her earnings were meagre and sometimes she earned nothing at all. She did not complain. Reluctantly, and always silently, she accepted the help offered by neighbours, but when she was not at home the neighbours, irritated by the whining, would run into the yard and stuff bread, vegetables, fruits—everything that could be eaten—into the insatiable mouth.

"Soon he will devour you altogether," they told her. "Why do you not give him away to some asylum, or hospital?"

"I gave birth to him," she would reply heavily. "I must feed him."

She was a handsome woman and more than one man sought her love, but all of them in vain, and to one for whom she cared more than the others, she said:

"I cannot be your wife, I am afraid to give birth to another monster. I do not want to disgrace you."

The man tried to persuade her. He reminded her that the Madonna is merciful to all mothers and looked upon them as Her own sisters, but the mother of the monster replied:

"I do not know what I have done, but see how cruelly I have been punished."

He pleaded with her, he wept and grew frantic, but she said: "No, I cannot go against my faith. Go!"

And he went away to some distant land and never returned.

And so for many years she provided food for that bottomless maw, those incessantly working jaws. He devoured the fruits of her labours, her blood and her life. His head grew steadily larger and more monstrous, like a huge ball that might at any moment detach itself from the weak, skinny neck and sail away over the houses, knocking against the corners and swaying lazily from side to side.

The stranger who chanced to look into the yard would stop, horrified by what he saw and unable to grasp its meaning. Beside the ivy-grown wall on a heap of stones as on some sacrificial altar stood the queer-shaped box with that monstrous head protruding from it; the yellow, wrinkled broad-featured face standing out against the green ivy would draw the gaze of the beholder and none who had seen it could soon forget those vacant staring eyes bulging out of their sockets, the broad flat nose, the abnormally developed cheek and jaw-bones, the quivering flaccid lips, revealing two rows of cruel teeth, the huge sensitive animal ears that seemed to live a life of their own—the entire hideous mask topped by a shock of black hair which curled in tiny ringlets like the hair of a Negro.

Clutching some bit of food in a hand as small and short as a lizard's claw he would tear at it with his teeth, jerking his head back and forth like a pecking bird and emitting loud grunting noises. Having eaten, he would look up at the people around him and bare his teeth, and then his eyes would focus on the bridge of his nose, merging in a murky thick splotch on a face contorted as if in a death agony. When hungry, he would stretch out his neck, open his red maw, and twisting his long, snake-like tongue, whine for food.

Onlookers would cross themselves and pray at the sight and turn away reminded suddenly of all the evil they had ever known, all the misfortune they had ever suffered.

Many times the dour old blacksmith remarked: "When I see that all-devouring mouth, I think that it is something like that has devoured my strength, and it seems to me that we all live and die for parasites."

That mute head evoked in everyone sorrowful thoughts and feelings from which the soul recoiled in horror.

The mother of the monster listened in silence to what was said about him. Her hair turned swiftly grey, her face grew lined, and she had long since forgotten how to laugh. People knew that at night she stood motionless by the door, staring up at the sky as if waiting for someone.

"What is it she waits for?" they asked one another.

"Put him on the square by the old church," her neighbours advised. "Foreigners pass there, they would not refuse to throw him a few coppers every day."

But the mother shuddered at the thought.

"It would be terrible to let men of other lands see him," she said. "What would they think of us?"

"There is poverty everywhere," they told her. "Everyone knows that!"

She shook her head.

But foreigners, driven by boredom, strolled about all over, the place peering into all the courtyards and, of course, one day they roamed into hers as well. She was home and she saw the grimaces of distaste and repugnance on the well-fed faces of these idle people. She heard them talk of her son, their mouths twisted into a leer, their eyes narrowed. Most painful to her were some words she overheard spoken in a tone of scorn, hostility and undisguised malice.

She memorized the foreign sounds, repeated them over and over to herself, for her heart—the heart of an Italian woman and a mother—sensed the insult they carried, and she went to a commissioner of her acquaintance and asked him what they meant.

"It depends on who said them," he replied, frowning. "They mean: 'Italy is dying out faster than the other Romanic races.' Where did you hear that lie ?"

She went away without replying.

The next day her son overate himself and died in convulsions.

She sat in the courtyard beside the box, with her hand on the lifeless head of her son, waiting calmly and looking questioningly into the eyes of all who came to her to look at the corpse.

No one spoke, no one asked her any questions, although perhaps many would have wished to congratulate her at her release from slavery, to say some word of comfort, for after all she had lost her son. But no one said anything. Sometimes people understand that there are things that are better left unsaid.

For a long time afterwards she continued to look at her neighbours with that unspoken question in her eyes, but in time she became as simple-hearted as they.

THE MOTHER OF A TRAITOR

Oɴᴇ ᴄᴀɴ ᴛᴀʟᴋ endlessly about Mothers.

For several weeks enemy hosts had surrounded the city in a tight ring of steel; by night fires were lit and the flames peered through the inky blackness at the walls of the city like a myriad of red eyes—they blazed malevolently, and their menacing glare evoked gloomy thoughts within the beleaguered city.

From the walls they saw the enemy noose draw tighter; saw the dark shadows hovering about the fires, and heard the neighing of well-fed horses, the clanging of weapons, the loud laughter and singing of men confident of victory—and what can be more jarring to the ear than the songs and laughter of the enemy?

The enemy had thrown corpses into all the streams that fed water to the city, he had burned down the vineyards around the walls, trampled the fields, cut down the orchards—the city was now exposed on all sides, and nearly every day the cannon and muskets of the enemy showered it with lead and iron.

Detachments of war-weary, half-starved soldiers trooped sullenly through the narrow streets of the city; from the windows of houses issued the groans of the wounded, the cries of the delirious, the prayers of women and the wailing of children. People spoke in whispers, breaking off in the middle of a sentence, tensely alert: was that not the enemy advancing?

Worst of all were the nights; in the nocturnal stillness the groans and cries were more distinctly audible; black shadows crept stealthily from the gorges of the distant mountains toward the half-demolished walls, hiding the enemy camp from view, and over the black ridges of the mountains rose the moon like a lost shield dented by sword blows.

And the people in the city, despairing of succour, worn out by toil and hunger, their hope of salvation waning from day to day, the people in the city stared in horror at that moon, at the sharp-toothed ridges of the mountains, the black maws of the gorges and the noisy camp of the enemy. Everything spoke to them of death, and not a star was there in the sky to give them consolation.

They were afraid to light the lamps in the houses, and a heavy darkness enveloped the streets, and in this darkness, like a fish stirring in the depths of a river, a woman draped from head to foot in a black cloak moved soundlessly.

When they saw her, people whispered to one another:

"Is it she?"

"It is she!"

And they withdrew into the niches under archways, or hurried past her with lowered heads. The patrol chiefs warned her sternly:

"Abroad again, Monna Marianna? Take care, you may be killed and nobody will bother to search for the culprit..."

She drew herself up and stood waiting, but the patrols passed by, either not daring or else scorning to raise their hand against her; the armed men avoided her like a corpse, and, left alone in the darkness, she continued her solitary wanderings from street to street, soundless and black like the incarnation of the city's misfortune, while all about her, as though pursuing her, melancholy sounds issued from the night: the groans, cries, prayers and the sullen murmur of soldiers who had lost all hope of victory.

A citizen and a mother, she thought of her son and her country: for at the head of the men who were destroying her town was her son, her gay, handsome, heartless son. Yet, not so long ago she had looked upon him with pride, regarding him as her precious gift to her country, a beneficent force she had brought forth to aid the people of the city where she herself had been born, where her son had been born and reared. Her heart was bound by hundreds of invisible threads to these ancient stones with which her forefathers had built their homes and raised the walls of the city; to the soil wherein lay buried the bones of her kinsfolk, to the legends, the songs and the hopes of the people. And now this heart had lost a loved one and it wept. She weighed in her heart as on scales her love for her son and her love for her native city, and she could not tell which weighed the more.

And so she wandered thus by night through the streets, and many, failing to recognize her, drew back in fear, mistaking her black figure for the incarnation of Death that was so near to all of them, and when they did recognize her, they turned silently away from the mother of a traitor.

But one day in a remote corner by the city walls she saw another woman, kneeling beside a corpse, so still that she seemed part of the earth. The woman was praying, her grief-stricken face upturned to the stars. And on the wall overhead the sentries spoke in low tones, their weapons grating against the stone.

The traitor's mother asked:

"Your husband?"

"No."

"Your brother?"

"My son. My husband was killed thirteen days ago, my son today."

And rising from her knees, the mother of the slain man said humbly:

"The Madonna sees all and knows all, and I am grateful to her!"

"For what?" asked the first, and the other replied:

"Now that he has died honourably fighting for his country I can say that I feared for him: he was light-hearted, too fond of revelry and I feared that he might betray his city, as did the son of Marianna, the enemy of God and Man, the leader of our foes, may he be accursed and the womb that bore him!"

Marianna covered her face and went on her way. The next morning she appeared before the city's defenders and said:

"My son has come to be your enemy. Either kill me or open the gates that I may go to him..."

They replied:

"You are a human being, and your country must be precious to you; your son is as much an enemy to you as to each one of us."

"I am his mother. I love him and feel that I am to blame for what he has become!"

Then they took counsel with one another and decided:

"It would not be honourable to kill you for the sins of your son. We know that you could not have led him to commit this terrible sin, and we can understand your distress. But the city does not need you even as a hostage; your son cares nought for you, we believe that he has forgotten you, fiend that he is, and there is your punishment if you think you have deserved it! We believe that is more terrible than death itself!"

"Yes," she said. "It is indeed more terrible."

And so they opened the gates and suffered her to leave the city and watched long from the battlements as she departed from her native soil, now drenched with the blood her son had spilt. She walked slowly, for her feet were reluctant to tear themselves away from this soil, and she bowed to the corpses of the city's defenders, kicking aside a broken weapon in disgust, for all weapons are abhorrent to mothers, save those that protect life.

She walked as though she carried a precious phial of water beneath her cloak and feared to spill a drop; and as her figure grew smaller and smaller to those who watched from the city wall, it seemed to them that with her went their dejection and hopelessness.

They saw her pause halfway and throwing back the hood of her cloak turn back and gaze long at the city. And over in the enemy's camp they saw her alone in the field and figures dark as her own approached her cautiously. They approached and inquired who she was and whence she had come.

"Your leader is my son," she said, and not one of the soldiers doubted it. They fell in beside her singing his praises, saying how clever and brave he was, and she listened to them with head proudly raised, showing no surprise, for her son could not be otherwise.

And now, at last, she stood before him whom she had known nine months before his birth, him whom she had never felt apart from her own heart. In silk and velvet he stood before her, his weapons studded with precious stones. All was as it should be, thus had she seen him so many times in her dreams—rich, famous and admired.

"Mother!" he said, kissing her hands. "Thou hast come to me, thou art with me, and tomorrow I shall capture that accursed city!"

"The city where thou wert born," she reminded him.

Intoxicated with his prowess, crazed with the thirst for more glory, he answered her with the arrogant heat of youth:

"I was born into the world and for the world, and I mean to make the world quake with wonder of me! I have spared this city for thy sake, it has been like a thorn in my flesh and has retarded my swift rise to fame. But now tomorrow I shall smash that nest of obstinate fools!"

"Where every stone knows and remembers thee as a child," she said.

"Stones are dumb, unless man makes them speak. Let the mountains speak of me, that is what I wish!"

"And what of men?" she asked.

"Ah yes, I have not forgotten them, mother. I need them too, for only in man's memory are heroes immortal!"

She said:

"A hero is he who creates life in defiance of death, who conquers death..."

"No!" he objected. "The destroyer is as glorious as

the builder of a city. See, we do not know who it was that built Rome—Aeneas or Romulus—yet we know well the name of Alaric and the other heroes who destroyed the city..."

"Which outlived all names," the mother reminded him.

Thus they conversed until the sun sank to rest; less and less frequently did she interrupt his wild speech, lower and lower sank her proud head.

A Mother creates, she protects, and to speak to her of destruction means to speak against her; but he did not know it, he did not know that he was negating her reason for existence.

A Mother is always opposed to death; the hand that brings death into the homes of men, is hateful and abhorrent to Mothers. But the son did not perceive this, for he was blinded by the cold glitter of glory that deadens the heart.

Nor did he know that a Mother can be as clever and ruthless as she is fearless, when the life she creates and cherishes is in question.

She sat with bowed head, and through the opening in the leader's richly appointed tent she saw the city where first she had felt the sweet tremor of life within her and the anguished convulsions of the birth of this child who now thirsted for destruction.

The crimson rays of the sun dyed the walls and towers of the city blood-red, cast a baleful glare on the window-panes so that the whole city seemed to be a mass of wounds with the crimson sap of life flowing from each gash. Presently the city turned black as a corpse and the stars shone above it like funeral candles.

She saw the dark houses where people feared to light candles so as not to attract the attention of the enemy, saw the streets steeped in gloom and rank with the stench of corpses, heard the muffled whispers of people awaiting death—she saw it all, all that was near and dear to her stood before her dumbly awaiting her decision, and she felt herself the mother of all those people in her city.

Clouds descended from the black peaks into the valley and swooped down like winged steeds upon the doomed city.

"We may attack tonight," said her son, "if the night is dark enough! It is hard to kill when the sun shines in your eyes and the glitter of the weapons blinds you, many a blow goes awry," he remarked, examining his sword.

The mother said to him:

"Come, my son, lay thy head on my breast and rest, remember how gay and kind thou wert as a child, and how everyone loved three..."

He obeyed her, laid his head in her lap and closed his eyes, saying:

"I love only glory and I love thee for having made me as I am."

"And women?" she asked bending over him.

"They are many, one tires of them as of everything that is too sweet."

"And dost thou not desire children?" she asked finally.

"What for? That they might be killed? Someone like me will kill them; that will give me pain and I shall be too old and feeble to avenge them."

"Thou art handsome, but as barren as a streak of lightning," she said with a sigh.

"Yes, like lightning..." he replied, smiling.

And he dozed there on his mother's breast like a child.

Then, covering him with her black cloak, she plunged a knife into his heart, and with a shudder he died, for who knew better than she were her son's heart beat. And, throwing his corpse at the feet of the astonished sentries, she said addressing the city:

"As a Citizen, I have done for my country all I could: as a Mother I remain with my son! It is too late for me to bear another, my life is of no use to anyone."

And the knife, still warm with his blood, her blood, she plunged with a firm hand into her own breast, and again she struck true, for an aching heart is not hard to find.

THE FISHERMAN'S BEHEST

THE CICADAS are strumming.

It is as if thousands of metal strings were stretched taut among the thick foliage of the olive-trees, the wind stirs the brittle leaves, they touch the strings and this light, ceaseless contact fills the air with intoxicating sound. It is not exactly music, yet it seems as if invisible hands were tuning hundreds of invisible harps, and one waits in tense expectancy for the tuning to cease, and for a grand string orchestra to strike up a triumphant hymn to the sun, sky and sea.

The wind blows, swaying the trees so that their

waving crowns seem to be moving from the mountains down to the sea. The surf beats dully and rhythmically against the rocky shore; the sea is a mass of living, white flecks of foam looking like great flocks of birds that have settled on its blue expanse. They all float in one direction, then disappear into the depths only to rise again with a faintly audible sound. And as though luring them away in their wake, two boats, their triple sails raised high, bob up and down on the horizon, like two grey birds themselves. The whole scene is as unreal as a distant, half-forgotten dream.

"There'll be a stiff gale by sundown!" says an old fisherman, sitting in the shadow of the rocks on the small pebbled beach.

The tide has washed bunches of brown, yellow and green seaweed on to the beach and it lies withering on the hot pebbles under the blazing sun, filling the salty air with the tangy scent of iodine. Curly wavelets chase one another up the beach.

The old fisherman resembles a bird with his small wizened face, his hooked nose and his round and doubt-less very sharp eyes hidden amid the dark folds of the skin. His gnarled, withered fingers lie motionless on his knees.

"About half a hundred years ago, signor," says the old man, in a voice that harmonizes with the murmur of the waves and the hum of the cicadas, "I remember just such a bright and glorious day, when everything seemed to laugh and sing. My father then was about forty, I was sixteen and in love, as is only natural for a lad of sixteen under a blessed sun like ours.

"'Come, Guido,' said my father, 'Let us go out for some pezzoni'; pezzoni, signor, is a very delicate tasty fish with pink fins, it is also known as coral fish because you find it deep down among the coral reefs. You catch it standing at anchor with a heavily weighted hook. And handsome fish.

"And so we set off anticipating nothing but a successful catch. My father was a strong man and an experienced fisherman, but shortly before this trip he had been ill, his chest ached and his fingers were twisted with rheumatism, the fisherman's disease.

"This is a very treacherous and evil wind that is blowing now so caressingly upon us from the shore, as if pushing us gently toward the sea. Out there it comes upon you unawares and suddenly hurls itself at you, as if you had done it an injury. It sends your barque flying, sometimes keel upwards with you in the water. It happens so quickly that before you have time to curse or to utter God's name you are sent swirling helplessly into the distance. A robber is more honest than that wind. But, then, men are always more honest than the elements.

"Well, it was just such a wind that struck us four kilometres from the shore, quite close by, as you see. It took us by surprise like a coward and a scoundrel.

"'Guido!' cried my father, seizing hold of the oar with his twisted hands. 'Hold on, Guido! Quick, the anchor!'

"But while I was fumbling for the anchor, the wind tore the oar out of my father's hand knocking him a blow on the chest that sent him reeling unconscious to the bottom of the boat. I had no time to help him, for every second threatened to capsize us. Everything happened very quickly: by the time I took up the oars we were being swept along, with the spray surrounding us on all sides, as the wind picked the crests off the waves and sprinkled us like the priest does, only with a great deal more energy and not in order to wash away our sins.

"'This is serious, my son!' said father, coming to his senses. He looked out toward the shore. 'This is going to be a long blow,' he said.

"When you are young you do not easily believe in danger; I tried desperately to row and did everything else that a sailor must do at critical moments, when the wind, the breath of wicked devils, is obligingly digging a thousand graves for you, and singing your requiem free of charge.

"'Sit still, Guido,' said my father, smiling and

shaking the water from his head. 'What's the use of digging at the sea with matchsticks? Save your strength or else the folks at home will await you in vain.'

"The green waves tossed our little craft as children toss a ball, they climbed over the sides, rose above our heads, roaring and shaking us madly; we dropped down into yawning pits, then climbed to the top of tall white peaks, and the shors sped swiftly farther and farther away and seemed to be dancing along with our barque.

"'You may return but I shall not!' my father said to me. 'Listen and I shall tell you what you must know about fishing and work...'

"And he began to tell me all he knew about the habits of one or another fish, where, when and how best to catch them.

"'Had we not better pray, father!' I suggested, when I saw how bad our plight was; we were like a couple of rabbits among a pack of white hounds that were baring their fangs at us from all sides.

"'God sees all!' said he. 'He knows that men whom He created to dwell on land are now perishing at sea and that one of them, having lost hope of salvation, must bequeath to his son all the knowledge he possesses. Work is necessary for the earth and for men. God understands that...'

"And when he had imparted to me all he knew about his craft, he told me what a man must know in order to live in peace with his fellow men.

"'Is this the time to teach me?' I said. 'On land you did not do it!'

"'On land death was never so close.'

"The wind howled like a wild beast, and the waves roared so loud that father had to shout for me to hear him.

"'Always behave towards men as if you were neither worse nor better than they, and that will be right! The nobleman and the fisherman, the priest and the soldier are part of the same body and you are as necessary a part of that body as all the others. Never approach a man thinking that there is more bad than good in him, believe that there is more good in him and you will always find it to be so. Men behave as one expects them to.'

"He did not say this all at once, of course. His words came to me through the spray and foam as we tossed from wave to wave, now plunging deep down, now climbing high up. Much of what he said was carried away by the wind before it reached me, much I did not understand, for, signor, how can one learn with death staring one in the face? I was afraid, I had never before seen the sea in such a fury or felt so helpless on it. And

I cannot say whether it was then or later on when I remembered those hours that I experienced a sensation I shall never forget as long as I live.

"I can see my father, as if it were yesterday, sitting at the bottom of the boat, his poor arms outstretched as he clung to the sides with his crooked, twisted fingers; his hat had been washed away and the waves struck against his head and his shoulders now from the right, now from the left, in front and behind, and each time he would toss his head, snort and shout to me. Drenched to the skin, he seemed to have shrunken in size and his eyes were large with fear, or perhaps with pain. With pain, I suppose.

"'Hark!' he would cry. 'Do you hear me?'

"Sometimes I would answer:

"'I hear you!'

"'Remember, all good comes from man.'

"'I shall remember!' I would reply.

"Never had he spoken thus to me on land. He had always been gay and kind but I had felt that he regarded me with amusement and distrust and that I was still a child to him. Sometimes this offended me, for youth is easily wounded.

"His shouts allayed my fear, perhaps that is why I remember everything so vividly."

The old fisherman fell silent, his eyes fixed on the

foamy sea. Then he smiled and went on with a wink:

"I have observed people for many years, signor, and I know that remembering is the same as understanding, and the more you understand the more good you see, that's the truth, believe me!

"There, I can remember his dear face, all wet and the big staring eyes looking at me gravely and lovingly and in such a way that I knew then I was not destined to die that day. I was afraid, but I knew I would not perish.

"Finally, of course, we capsized. There we were both in the seething water, with the foam blinding us, the waves hurling our bodies about, dashing them against the keel of the boat. We had lashed to the thwarts everything that could be tied, in our hands we held the ropes, we would not be cast away from our barque so long as we had the strength to hold on, but it was hard to keep our heads above water. Several times he and I were thrown against the keel and washed off again. The worst of it is that your head swims, you are deafened and blinded, your ears fill with water, and you swallow great quantities of it.

"This lasted for a long time, about seven hours, until the wind suddenly turned, blowing strongly shoreward, and we were carried swiftly toward the land.

"'Hold on!' I cried joyfully.

Father shouted something back but I heard only one word:

"'...rocks.'

"He was thinking of the rocks on the shore, but they were still far off and I did not heed him. But he knew better than I, we were borne along numb and helpless amid the mountains of water, clinging like snails to our boat which knocked us about unmercifully. This went on for a long while but at last the dark crags of the coast came into view. After that everything happened very swiftly. Swaying, they moved toward us, bending over the water, ready to crash down upon us. The white waves hurled our bodies forward once, twice, our boat crunched like a nut under the heel of a boot, I was torn loose, saw the black ribs of the rocks as sharp as knives looming before me, saw my father's head high above mine, then lifted above those devil's claws. He was picked up an hour or two later with his back broken and his skull smashed. The wound in his head was so big that part of the brain had been washed out of it, and I can remember the grey chunks of matter in the wound with red veins running through it like marble or foam mixed with blood. His body was terribly mutilated, but his face was clear and calm and his eyes tightly closed.

"I ? Yes, I was also badly battered up, I was un-conscious when they pulled me ashore. We had been carried away to the mainland beyond Amalfi, a long way from home, but, of course, the folk there are also fishermen and such things do not surprise them but make them kind and gentle. Men who lead a dangerous life are always kind!

"I'm afraid I haven't been able to describe the feeling that last talk with my father gave me, the feeling I have been carrying in my heart for fifty-one years now. You need special words for that, not words but music perhaps. But we fishermen are as simple as the fish, we cannot talk as well as we would like! We feel and know so much more than we can express.

"The important thing is that he, my father, in his hour of death, knowing that he could not escape it, was not afraid, he did not forget about me, his son, and he found the strength and the time to pass on to me every-thing he thought I should know. I have lived for sixty-seven years and I can say that all that he told me then is the truth!"

The old man took off his knitted cap that had once been red and was now brown, pulled out his pipe and bending his naked, bronzed skull, said emphatically:

"Yes, it is all true, dear signor! Men are as you wish to see them, look at them in kindness and you will do good both to them and to yourself. They will become better, and you too. It is simple, isn't it?"

The wind rose steadily, the waves mounted higher, grew sharper and whiter; flocks of birds scurried farther and farther into the distance, and the two boats with the three rows of sails had already disappeared behind the blue rim of the horizon.

The steep shores of the island were white with foam, the dark-blue water was agitated, and the cicadas kept up their tireless, passionate din.

THE SENTENCE

THE SIROCCO was blowing that day, a moist wind from Africa, an evil wind! It irritates the nerves and puts men in an ill humour. That is why the two cabbies, Giuseppe Cirotta and Luigi Meta, quarrelled. The quarrel broke out suddenly, no one knew who started it, but people saw Luigi hurl himself at Giuseppe and try to seize him by the throat, and Giuseppe, draw in his head to hide his thick red neck and put up a pair of black heavy fists.

They were pulled apart at once.

"What is the matter?" people asked.

Luigi, his face black with rage, shouted: "Let that ox repeat what he said of my wife!"

Cirotta tried to get away, he hid his little eyes in the folds of a contemptuous grimace and shaking his round black head refused te repeat the insult. Whereupon Meta said in a loud voice:

"He says that he has known the sweetness of my wife's embraces!"

"Oho!" murmured the onlookers. "That is no joke, that is a serious matter. Calm yourself, Luigi! You are a stranger here, but your wife is one of us, we know her from childhood, and if you have been wronged, the shadow of her offence falls on all of us. Let us be just!"

Then they turned on Cirotta.

"Did you say that?"

"Yes, I did," he confessed.

"Is it true?"

"Has anyone ever known me to lie?"

Cirotta was a decent man, a good husband and father. This was an ugly business. The people were silent and dismayed. Luigi went home and said to his wife Concetta:

"I am leaving you. I want to have nothing more to do with you unless you can prove that this scoundrel's accusation is false."

She wept, of course, but tears do not prove anything. Luigi thrust her away from him, and left

124

her with an infant in arms, and no money or bread.

Then the women intervened, first of all Caterina, the vegetable vendor, a clever fox of a wench, with a body like an old sack stuffed with flesh and bones and badly crumpled in spots.

"Signori," said Caterina, "you have heard it said that this affair touches the honour of all of us. This is not a matter of a little fun on a moonlight night. The fate of two mothers is at stake. Right? I shall take Concetta to my house and she shall live with me until we discover the truth."

And so it was. After a while Caterina and that old hag Lucia, whose voice can be heard three miles away, got to work on poor Giuseppe. They called him in and commenced to poke their fingers into his soul as if it were some old rag.

"Now then, man, tell us, how many times did you embrace Concetta?"

The fat Giuseppe puffed out his cheeks, pondered a while and said:

"Once."

"You could say that without stopping to think," remarked Lucia, as if to herself.

"Did it happen in the evening, at night or in the morning?" Caterina persisted, for all the world like a magistrate.

Giuseppe chose the evening without hesitation.

"Was it still light?"

"Yes," the simpleton replied.

"So! Then you could see her body?"

"Certainly!"

"Very well then, describe it to us."

But he saw whither the questions were leading and he opened his mouth like a sparrow that has choked on a grain of barley, started to mutter and grew so angry that his huge ears turned purple.

"What do you want met to say?" he growled. "Do you think I examined her like a doctor?"

"Aha, so you eat the fruits without admiring them?" said Lucia. "But perhaps you noticed one particular thing about Concetta?" she urged him with an evil wink.

"It all happened so quickly," said Giuseppe, "that I swear I didn't notice anything."

"Then that proves you never had her!" cried Caterina. She is a kind-hearted old woman but she can be very stern when she pleases. In a word, they led him into such a maze of contradictions that the fellow finally hung his foolish head and confessed: "There wasn't anything at all. I made it up out of spite."

The old women were not surprised.

"We knew it," they declared and sending him away, they left the affair to the judgement of the menfolk.

The next day our workingmen's association met. Cirotta stood before them charged with libelling a woman, and old Giacomo Fasca, the blacksmith, made a fine speech:

"Citizens, comrades, good men! If we expect to be treated with justice ourselves, we must be just toward one another. Let all men know that we appreciate the value of what we demand and that justice is not an empty word for us as it is for our masters. Here is a man who has libelled a woman, insulted a comrade, broken up one family and brought misery to another, forcing his own wife to suffer from jealousy and shame. We must be severe with him. What shall we do with him?"

Sixty-seven tongues pronounced in unison:

"Expel him from our community!"

But fifteen held that this was too harsh a measure, and a dispute arose. They shouted themselves hoarse—after all the fate of a human being was being decided, and not of one human being, for after all he was married, he had three children—what crime had his wife and children committed? He had a house, a vineyard, a pair of horses, four donkeys for foreigners—all this he had earned by his own labour, and he had laboured much. Poor Giuseppe sat alone in the corner, as black as the devil, hunched up on his chair, his head bent, kneading his hat in his hands. He had already torn off the ribbon and was now working on the brim, and his fingers danced like the fingers of a fiddler. And when they asked him if he had anything to say, he got to his feet with difficulty and said:

"I ask for clemency! None of us is sinless. It would not be fair to drive me away from the land where I have lived for more than thirty years, the land on which my forefathers toiled!"

The women were also opposed to banishment, and finally Fasca suggested this course:

"I believe, friends, that he will be well punished if we compel him to support Luigi's wife and child. Let him pay her half of what Luigi earned!"

There was a good deal more argument, but finally they chose this way out and Giuseppe Cirotta felt that he had got off easily. Indeed everyone was satisfied, we had settled the affair among ourselves, without recourse to court or dagger. We do not like, signor, when our affairs are described in the language of the newspapers where the words you can understand are as rare as teeth in the mouth of an old man. Nor do we like when judges, who are strangers to us and understand very little of life, speak of us as though we were savages and they the Lord's angels who have never tasted wine and fish and never touched a woman. We are simple people and we look at life simply.

So it was decided: Giuseppe Cirotta was to provide for Luigi's wife and their child. But the matter did not end there. When Luigi learned that Cirotta had lied and that this signora was innocent, and when he was told of our sentence, he wrote and invited her to join him.

"Come to me and we will be happy together again," he wrote. "Do not take a single centesimo from that man, and if you have already taken something, throw it back in his face! I have not wronged you, how could I know that that man could lie in such a thing as love?"

To Cirotta he wrote another letter:

"I have three brothers and all four of us have vowed to kill you like a ram if ever you leave the island and turn up in Sorrento, Castellamare, Torre or anywhere else. As soon as we find out that you have left we shall kill you, remember! This is as true as that the men of your community are good honest men. My signora does not need your help, even my pig would refuse your bread. Live, but do not dare to leave the island until I say you may."

They say Cirotta took that letter to our magistrate to find out whether Luigi could not be sent to prison for threatening his life. And the judge is believed to have said:

"Yes, we can send him to prison but then his brothers

would be sure to kill you. They would come here and murder you. I advise you to wait. That will be better. Anger is not like love, it does not last very long..."

The judge might have said that. He is a good, kind man and he writes quite good verse too, but I do not believe Cirotta went to him with that letter. No, Cirotta is a decent fellow at heart and he would never be guilty of such a piece of tactlessness. After all, he would be laughed to scorn if ever his comrades found out.

We are simple working folk, signor, we have our own way of life, our own ideas and opinions. We have the right to live as we please, as we think best.

Socialists? O, my friend, every working man is born a Socialist, I believe, and though we do not read books we have a good nose for the truth—for truth always smells of working man's sweat!

HOW GIOVANNI BECAME A SOCIALIST

Beside the door of the white cantina hidden among the thick shrubbery of an old vineyard two men, Vincenzo, the house-painter, and Giovanni, the turner, are sitting over a jug of wine. Their table stands in the shade of a canopy of grape vines intertwined with convolvulus and tiny Chinese roses. The painter is a small, dark, bony man. His black eyes are lit up by the gentle smile of the dreamer, and that smile gives his face a naïve, childlike expression in spite of the dark blue of his close-shaven upperlip and cheeks. He has a small, sweet, girlish mouth and long hands. His restless fingers are playing with a golden blossom. He presses it to his full lips and closes his eyes.

"It is possible," he says softly. "I do not know." He shakes his long, narrow head and his reddish curls fall on to his tall forehead.

"Yes, yes! The farther north you go, the tougher the people!" insists Giovanni. He is a young man with a large head, broad shoulders and a shock of black curly hair. His face is copper-coloured, his sunburned nose has a scaly white layer of peeling skin, his eyes are the large, gentle eyes of an ox. The thumb of his left hand is missing. His speech is as slow as the movement of his hands, which are stained deep with machine oil and iron dust. Squeezing his wine glass in his dark fingers with the broken nails, he continues in his deep bass:

"Milan, Turin—these are splendid workshops where new men are being moulded, where a new mentality is arising! Wait, before very long the world will grow honest and wise!"

"Yes," said the little painter, and lifting his glass to catch the sunbeam, he began to sing:

> Oh, how warm is the earth in the morn of our days,
> But alas, we grow old and the gentle warmth fades.

"The farther north you go, I say, the better the

work. The French are not as lazy as we are, then come the Germans, and finally, the Russians. There is a people for you!"

"Yes!"

"Downtrodden and oppressed, at the risk of losing their freedom and their lives, they have done great things. It is thanks to them that the whole East has sprung to life!"

"A land of heroes!" said the painter, bending his head. "I wish I lived there..."

"You!" exclaimed the turner, slapping his knee with the side of his hand. "You would be a lump of ice in a week!"

Both laughed heartily.

Flowers of blue and gold bloomed around them, sunbeams quivered in the air, the Almandine wine sparkled in the glass jug, and from the distance came the whispering sound of the sea.

"Now listen, my good Vincenzo," said the turner with a broad smile, "and I shall tell you how I became a Socialist. You must put it in verse. Do you know the story?"

"No," said the painter, pouring the wine into the glass and smiling at the red stream. "You have never told me. That skin of yours sits so well on your bones, that I thought you were born in it!"

"It was born as naked and foolish as you and all other men. In my youth I dreamed of marrying a rich woman. When I was in the army I worked hard to become an officer. I was twenty-three when I began to feel that all is not well in this world and that it was a shame to go on being a fool."

The painter leaned his elbows on the table, raised his head and gazed up at the hill and the great pines waving their branches at the very top.

"My unit was sent to Bologna. The peasants there were making trouble, some were demanding lower rents, others wanted higher pay. It thought both sides were in the wrong. To reduce land rents and raise wages was absurd, in my opinion. Why, the landlords would be ruined! To a towndweller like myself it all seemed stupid and senseless. Moreover I was very angry, what with the heat, the constant moving from place to place, and the sentry duty at night—because those fellows were smashing the landlords' machines, burning grain and wrecking everything that did not belong to them."

He drank his wine in tiny sips, and, warming to his subject, he went on:

"They went about the fields in dense droves like sheep, but sullen and silent. They meant business. We dispersed them, showing our bayonets, sometimes pushing them with our rifle butts. But they did not take fright, they scattered slowly and gathered again. It got to be as boring as High Mass, and it dragged on from day to day like the fever. Luoto, our corporal, a nice chap from Abruzzi and a peasant himself, felt very badly about the whole thing. He grew thin and haggard and looked very miserable.

"'It's bad, my children!' he would say. 'It looks as if we shall have to use our rifles, damn it!'

"His croaking upset us even more, and to make matters worse, there were those pigheaded peasants poking their heads around every corner, every hill and every tree, glaring at us with hatred in their eyes. Naturally they didn't feel any too friendly toward us."

"Drink!" said little Vincenzo, pushing a full glass toward his friend.

"Thanks, and here's to staunch men!" cried the turner. He tossed off his drink, wiped his moustache with his hand and continued:

"One day I was standing on a knoll near an olive grove guarding the trees—because the peasants wrecked them whenever they had a chance. Two peasants, an old man and a youth, were digging a ditch at the bottom of the hill. It was very hot, the sun burnt like fire—one of those days when a man wishes he were a fish. I watched the two at work, feeling bored and angry. At midday they stopped working and got out some bread and cheese and a jug of wine. The devil take you, I thought to myself. Suddenly the old man, who had not once glanced in my direction until then, said something to the lad. The lad shook his head and the old man shouted:

"'Go, I tell you!' in a stern voice.

"The young man came over to me with the jug, and said none too graciously: 'My father thinks you are thirsty and offers you some wine!'

"It was awkward, but pleasant. I declined the offer, nodded to the old man and thanked him, but he said, looking up at the sky:

"'Drink, signor, drink! We are offering it to the man and not the soldier. We do not expect our wine to make the soldier kinder.'"

"'You needn't bite, damn you!' I said to myself, and took a swallow of wine and thanked them, and they began to eat down there. Before long Hugo—he was from Salerno—came to relieve me, and I told him that those two peasants were all right. That evening as I was standing by the door of the shed where the machines were kept, some tiles fell off the roof, one hit my head, but not hard, and another one struck my left shoulder so violently that my arm went numb."

The turner began to laugh, opening his mouth wide and screwing up his eyes.

"In those days and in that place," he said, through his laughter, "tiles, stones and sticks lived a life of their own, and the violence of inanimate objects earned us some nice bumps on our heads. A soldier would be going somewhere or standing still and suddenly a stick would spring up from the ground and strike him, or a stone would drop down from the skies. It made us furious of course."

A sad look came into the eyes of the little house-painter, his face grew pale and he said softly:

"It is always painful to hear of such things..."

"It can't be helped. People learn very slowly. But to get on with my story. I called for help and I was carried into a house. One of our fellows was lying there. His face had been cut open with a stone and when I asked him how it had happened he said, with a wry smile:

"'An old woman, my comrade, an old grey-haired witch struck me and then invited me to kill her!'

"'Was she arrested?'" I asked him.

"'No. I said I had fallen and hurt myself. The commander did not believe me, of course. I could tell by the way he looked at me. But how could I admit that an old woman had injured me? The devil take it! Theirs is a hard life, and I can understand why they hate us.'"

"'So that's it,' I thought. Presently a doctor arrived and two ladies with him. One was a very beautiful lady with fair hair, a Venetian I believe, the other I don't remember. They examined my shoulder—it was a trifle of course—applied a compress and went away."

The turner frowned, fell silent and rubbed his hands. His friend refilled the glasses, holding the wine jug high as he poured so that the vivid red stream of wine quivered in the air.

"My comrade and I were sitting by the window," the turner went on gloomily. "We sat in the shade out of the sun and we heard the sweet voice of that fair lady as she and her friend strolled in the garden with the doctor. They spoke French, which I understand quite well.

"'Did you notice his eyes?' I heard her say. 'He is a peasant too, of course, and perhaps when he discards his uniform he will also be a Socialist like all the others. To think that men with eyes like that want to conquer the whole world, to change everything, to drive us all out and destroy us. And all in the name of some blind, stupid justice!'

"'Foolish lads,' said the doctor, 'half children, half animals.'

"'Animals—yes! But what is there childlike about them?'

"'Oh, those dreams of universal equality...'

"'Think of it,' she cried, 'I, the equal of that fellow with the ox eyes, and that other with the face of a bird, all of us, you and I and she, equals of them, these people of common blood! Men who can be hired to kill others of their own kind, animals like themselves...'

"She spoke a great deal, and with much heat and I listened and thought to myself: 'Ah, signora!' I had seen her before, and you know how passionately a soldier can dream of a woman. Naturally I had imagined her to be kind and warm-hearted, and clever too, for in those days I believed that all people of the upper classes must be remarkably clever.

"I asked my comrade whether he understood what they were saying. But he knew no French. And when I told him what the blonde lady had said, he grew very angry. He sprang up and began pacing the room, his eyes flashing, or rather his eye, for the other was bandaged up.

"'So that is how it is!' he fumed. 'She uses me but does not consider me a human being! For her sake I suffer the humiliation of soldiery, and she dares to trample on my self-esteem. She denies me the right to human dignity. For the sake of protecting her property I risk losing my soul...'

"He was not a stupid fellow and he felt himself deeply insulted. I too. The next day we talked openly about that lady, without mincing words. Luoto only muttered under his breath and advised us to take care.

"'Do not forget, my children, that you are soldiers and there is such a thing as discipline!'

"We had not forgotten. But from that day on many of us, indeed nearly all of us, to say the truth, became deaf and blind, and those peasants were not slow to take advantage of our sudden infirmities. They won their fight. They began to be very friendly toward us. That blonde lady might have learned much from them. For instance, they would have taught her how honest men should be treated. When at last we were withdrawn from that place where we had come with the intention of spilling blood, many of us received gifts of flowers. As we marched down the village street they pelted us with flowers, my friend, and not stones and tiles! I believe we had earned those flowers. We could forget the unfriendly welcome we had received with such a splendid send-off!"

He laughed, and then said: "There, Vincenzo, make a poem of that..."

The painter, with a thoughtful smile, replied:

"Yes, it is fit material for a poem! I believe I can do it. When a man passes the age of twenty-five love poems no longer come easily."

He threw aside the flower, now withered, plucked another and glancing over his shoulder, went on in a low voice:

"When a man has traversed the path from his mother's breast to the breast of his beloved, he must strive for another kind of happiness."

His companion, shaking the wine in his glass, said nothing. The sea murmured softly down below and the scent of the flowers floated in the warm air.

"It is the sun that makes us too lazy, too soft," muttered the turner.

"I cannot write good love verse any more, I am very displeased with myself," said Vincenzo, knitting his delicate brows.

"Have you thought of something?"

The painter did not reply at once.

"Yes," he said at last. "It came to me yesterday, on the roof of the Como Hotel."

And he began to recite in a low, lilting voice:

> The shore is deserted, the late autumn sun
> Bids a tender farewell to the ancient grey rocks.
> The hungry waves hurl themselves on the dark boulders

Washing the bright sun into the cold blue sea.
And the copper-hued leaves, torn loose by the autumn winds,
Gleam in the foam of the tide, like the bright corpses of birds,
The sad pale sky looks down on the angry sea.
Only the sun laughs as slowly it sinks to rest.

There was a long pause; the painter bowed his head looking down at the ground. The burly turner smiled.

"One can write well of many things, but best of all about man, the song of good men!"

BROTHER AND SISTER

A GOLDEN SHOWER of sunlight streams through the dark-green curtain of vines on to the hotel terrace—threads of gold strung on the air. Shadows of weird design lie on the grey flagged floor and the white tablecloths, and it seems that if you looked at them long enough you might learn to read them as one would read a poem. Clusters of grapes glow in the sunshine like pearls or that strange, lustreless stone, the olivine, and in the carafe of water on the table there are blue diamonds.

A tiny lace handkerchief lies on the floor between

the tables. A lady dropped it, of course, and doubtless she was divinely beautiful. How could it be otherwise, how could one think otherwise on this serene day full of languorous heat, a day when everything commonplace and dull vanishes before the sun's glory as if hiding in shame.

All is still; the only sounds are the twittering of the birds in the garden, the humming of the bees over the flowers and the faint sigh of a song coming from the vineyards somewhere in the hills. There are two singers—a man and a woman, and each verse is separated from the next by a minute of silence, which lends a peculiar prayer-like quality to the song.

And now a lady appears, slowly ascending the broad marble staircase leading from the garden. An old lady, very tall, with a dark, stern face, knitted brows and thin lips obstinately compressed as if she had just said: "No!" Over her bony shoulders she wears a long, wide cape-like mantle of gold-tinted silk edged with lace, a black lace scarf covers her small grey head, in one hand she carries a red parasol with a long handle, and in the other, a black velvet handbag sewn with silver thread. She marches through the gossamer web of sunbeams with the firm tread of a soldier, and her parasol taps loudly on the flagstones of the terrace. In profile her face is even more austere: the nose is hooked, the chin with a large grey wart on it is sharp, the bulging forehead overhangs dark sockets in which the eyes are hidden among a fine network of wrinkles, set so deeply that the old woman seems to be blind.

After her, waddling from side to side like a duck, appears a squat figure of a hunchback with a soft grey hat on his large drooping head. His hands are hidden in the pockets of his waistcoat, and this makes him look even wider and more angular than he is. He wears a white suit and white boots with soft soles. His mouth is half-open revealing yellow, uneven teeth, a few dark bristly hairs stick out unpleasantly on his upper lip, he breathes quickly and painfully, his nose quivers but his moustache does not move. His short legs twist horribly as he walks, and his huge eyes stare dully down at the ground. His small body is bedecked with a host of large objects: he wears a large gold cameo ring on the forefinger of his left hand, a large golden medallion is suspended from the end of the black ribbon that serves as a watch chain, and in his blue tie is an oversized opal, the unlucky stone.

Still another figure emerges on the terrace, also an old woman, small and round with a red kindly face and lively eyes, a jolly, garrulous body no doubt.

They cross the terrace to the door of the hotel

like figures from a painting by Hogarth: unsightly, sad, comical and so alien to everything under this radiant sun that the world seems to turn dim and pale at the sight of them.

They are Hollanders, a brother and sister, children of a diamond merchant and banker, and theirs is a curious history, if one is to believe the tale that is told of them.

As a child, the hunchback had been quiet, shy and thoughtful, caring nothing for toys or games. No one paid much attention to this expect his sister; his father and mother believed that such behaviour was natural for an unfortunate creature, but the little girl, who was four years his senior, was disturbed by her brother's strange ways.

She spent nearly all her time with him, trying to amuse him, to make him laugh. She gave him toys to play with and he piled them up one atop the other, pyramid fashion. Rarely did she see him smile; usually he regarded her with the same dull, blank expression in his large eyes with which he stared at everything about him. That look irritated her.

"Don't you dare to look at me like that, you'll grow up to be an imbecile!" she would cry, stamping her feet. She would pinch him and slap him and he would whimper and throw up his long thin arms to protect his head, but he never ran away from her and never complained to anyone.

Later on, when she thought that he would be able to understand what was perfectly clear to her, she tried to reason with him:

"If you are deformed you must be clever otherwise we shall all be ashamed of you—papa, mama and everybody! Even the servants will be ashamed to serve in a rich house that has a little cripple in it. In a rich house everything must be either beautiful or clever, understand?"

"Yes," he replied gravely, tilting his large head to one side and turning his dark, lifeless stare on her.

The father and mother were delighted by the little girl's attitude to her brother, they praised her kind heart in his presence, and gradually she became the acknowledged companion of the little hunchback. She taught him to use his toys, helped him with his lessons and read him stories about princes and fairies.

But he continued to pile up his toys into tall heaps as though he strove to reach up to something, and took little interest in his lessons. Only the wondrous deeds of fairy-tale characters brought a faint smile to his lips, and one day he asked his sister:

"Are princes ever hunchbacked?"

"No."

"And knights?"

"Of course not!"

The boy sighed wearily, and his sister, laying her hand on his coarse hair, said:

"But wise magicians are always hunchbacks."

"Then I shall be a magician," he said meekly, and added after a thoughtful pause:

"Fairies are always beautiful, aren't they?"

"Always."

"Like you?"

"Perhaps! But even more beautiful I think," she said honestly.

When he was eight years old his sister noticed that whenever they walked or drove past building sites the boy's face would light up with wonder and he would watch the men working with rapt attention, and then turn to her with a questioning look in his dull eyes.

"Does that interest you?" she asked him.

"Yes," he replied.

"Why?"

"I do not know."

But one day he explained: "Such little men and such little bricks, and what great houses they make. Is that how the whole city was made?"

"Of course."

"Our house too?"

"Certainly."

Glancing at him, she said firmly: "You are going to be a famous architect when you grow up!"

They bought him a great quantity of wooden blocks, and from that time a fierce passion for building flared up in him. For days on end he would sit on the floor of his room silently building tall towers, and when they tumbled down with a crash he built them up again. This came to be such a necessity for him that even at mealtime he would try to build something out of knives, forks and napkin rings. His eyes grew deeper and more concentrated, his hands came to life and were constantly in motion, and his fingers explored every object within his reach.

Now, during his walks through the city, he would have liked to stand for hours watching houses being built, seeing them rise slowly from the ground toward the sky. With quivering nostrils he greedily inhaled the brick dust and the smell of the boiling lime, his eyes grew sleepy and a film of dreamy thoughtfulness came over them, and when he was told that it was not nice to stand and stare he seemed not to hear.

"Come!" his sister urged, pulling him by the hand. He would bend his head and move on, turning back again and again.

"You are going to be an architect, aren't you?" his sister asked him again and again.

"Yes."

One day, as they were sitting in the drawing-room after dinner waiting for coffee, the father observed that it was time the boy stopped playing with toys and began to study in real earnest, but his sister spoke up in the tone of one whose opinion must needs be reckoned with:

"It trust, papa, that you are not thinking of sending him to some school?"

The father, a large, clean-shaven man with a vast amount of sparkling jewellery distributed about his person, lit a cigar.

"And why not, pray?"

"You know very well why."

Since they were speaking of him, the hunchback slipped out of the room, and as he went he heard his sister say:

"But everyone will make fun of him!"

"Ah yes, of course!" said the mother in a voice as raw as the autumn wind.

"People like him must be hidden away!" the sister said passionately.

"Ah yes, there is nothing to be proud of," said the mother. "What a clever little head it is to be sure!"

"I daresay you are right," the father agreed.

"But, how clever she is!"

The hunchback turned in the doorway and said: "I am not stupid either, you know . . ."

"That remains to be seen," said the father, and the mother observed: "No one thinks you are . . ."

"You shall study at home," declared the sister, making him sit down beside her. "You shall learn everything an architect needs to know. Will you like that ?"

"Yes. You will see."

"What shall I see ?"

"What I like."

She was only slightly taller than he, about half a head, but to him she seemed to tower high above everyone else, including mother and father. She was fifteen at that time. He resembled a crab, while she— slim, tall and strong—seemed to him like a lovely fairy who held the entire house and himself under her spell.

And now the hunchback began to be visited regularly by cold, polite people who tried to teach him something, explaining patiently and asking him questions, but he admitted unabashed that he understood nothing of what his teachers said, and stared coldly through them thinking his own thoughts. He spoke little, but sometimes he asked strange questions:

"What happens to people who do not want to do anything?"

His teacher, a man with perfect manners, dressed in a black coat buttoned up to the throat and resembling at once a priest and a soldier, replied:

"The worst things imaginable happen to such people! For instance, many of them become Socialists."

"Thank you," said the hunchback; he treated his teacher with the dry courtesy of an adult. "And what is a Socialist?"

"At best he is a dreamer and an idler, in general a mental cripple with no conception of God, property or country."

His teachers always replied briefly and their answers embedded themselves in his memory like cobble-stones in the pavement.

"Can an old woman be a mental cripple as well?"

"Of course..."

"And a little girl too?"

"Yes. It is something one is born with..."

His teachers said of him: "He has very little ability for mathematics, but shows great interest in questions of morality."

"You talk too much," his sister told him when she learned of his conversations with his teachers.

"They talk more than I do."

"You don't pray to God enough."

"He won't cure my hump..."

"Oh, so that is what you are thinking of now?" she exclaimed in amazement. "I forgive you this time," she declared, "but you must banish such thoughts from your mind for ever, you hear?"

"Yes."

By this time she was wearing long dresses, and he had turned thirteen.

From that day the hunchback began to give his sister much trouble. She rarely entered his work room without some board, plank or tool falling on her shoulder, her head on her fingers. The hunchback always shouted a warning to her: "Look out!" But he was always a moment late and she was often hurt.

Once, limping with pain, she rushed over to him pale with anger and shouted: "You are doing this on purpose, monster!" and she struck him on the face.

His legs were weak and he fell, and sitting there on the floor he said softly without tears or resentment: "How can you think that? You love me, do you not? You do love me?"

She ran away, groaning with pain. Later she came back to apologize.

"You see," she explained, "you never did that before..."

"I didn't have all this before," he replied calmly with a sweeping gesture which included the entire room with boards stacked in the corners, wood piled high on the carpenter's bench and a lathe by the wall, all in great confusion.

"Why have you dragged all this rubbish in here?" she asked him, glancing around her with disgust and suspicion.

"You will see!"

He had already began to build. He had made a rabbit hutch and a kennel for the dog, and was now working on a new kind of rat-trap. His sister eagerly followed the progress of his work and at mealtimes she boasted proudly of his success to their mother and father. The father nodded with approval.

"Everything begins with the little things, that is how it is always!" he said.

And the mother, embracing her daughter, said to her son: "Do you realize how much you owe her?"

"Yes," replied the hunchback.

When the rat-trap was finished he called his sister and showed her the clumsy contraption.

"This is no toy, you know," he said. "It can be patented! See how simple it is and how powerful. Put your finger here."

The girl touched it, something snapped. She screamed

and the hunchback jumped up and down beside her muttering: "Oh, oh, it's the wrong one, the wrong one..."

The mother came running, and then the servants. They took the trap apart and released the girl's squashed blue finger and carried her away in a dead faint.

That evening his sister summoned him and asked: "You did that on purpose. You hate me. Why?"

Shaking his hump, he replied in a low, calm voice:

"You touched it with the wrong hand, that's all."

"That's a lie!"

"But... but why should I try to disfigure your hand? Besides, it wasn't even the hand you struck me with..."

"Take care, cripple, you cannot outwit me!"

"I know that," he agreed.

His angular face was as calm as usual; his eyes were thoughtful, it was impossible to believe that he was angry or that he could be lying.

After that she did not go to his rooms quite so often. Her friends came to see her, vivacious young girls in bright-coloured gowns, who flitted lightly through the large, rather chill and austere rooms, and the pictures, statues, flowers and gilt ornaments all seemed to grow warmer in their presence. Sometimes his sister brought them to his room—they primly gave him their little fingers with the pink nails, touching his hand cautiously as if they feared to break it. They talked to him very gently and they stared with interest not unmixed with curiosity at the sight of the hunchback among his tools, drawings, chunks of wood and shavings. He knew that these girls called him "the inventor," his sister had seen to that, and that they all expected him to do something in the future that would bring fame to his father's name. His sister always spoke of this with such assurance.

"He is ugly, of course, but he is very clever," she often said.

She was nineteen now, and already had a suitor when her father and mother lost their lives during a trip on a pleasure yacht which was rammed and sunk by the drunken helmsman of an American freighter. She too was to have gone on that yacht but she had remained home with a toothache.

When the news of her parents' death reached her she forgot her toothache and rushed up and down the room, weeping and wringing her hands:

"No, no, it cannot be, it cannot be!"

The hunchback, standing by the door with the curtain wrapped about him, regarded her with a fixed stare and shaking his hump, he said:

"Father was so round and so empty I cannot understand how he could possibly drown..."

"Keep quiet, you do not love anyone!" cried his sister.

"I simply do not know how to say sweet words," he said.

The father's body was never found, but the mother had died before she reached the water and her body was recovered. She lay in her coffin just as she had been in life—as dry and brittle as the dead branch of an old tree.

"You and I are all alone now," the sister said sorrowfully to her brother after the mother's funeral, regarding him with her cold grey eyes. "It will be hard for us. We do not know anything and we may lose much. What a pity I cannot get married at once!"

"Oh!" exclaimed the hunchback.

"What do you mean by that?"

He thought for a moment, then said: "We are alone."

"You say that as if it pleased you!"

"Nothing pleases me."

"That too is a great pity. You are so unlike a living person!"

In the evenings her fiancé would come to see her—a lively little man, with fair hair, round sunburned face and a bushy moustache. He laughed incessantly all evening long and no doubt could laugh all day as well. They were already betrothed and a house was being built for them in one of the best streets in the city. The hunchback had never been at that building site and did not like to hear it spoken of. His sister's fiancé would slap him on the shoulder with his small pudgy ringed hand and, with a smile that showed a mouth full of small teeth, would say: "You ought to come and have a look at it, eh? What do you think?"

For a long time the hunchback refused on diverse pretexts, but finally he gave in and went with his sister and her fiancé to the site. The two men climbed the scaffolding, but when they reached the top they fell. The fiancé fell straight into a vat of lime, but the brother's clothes caught on a protruding board and he was suspended in mid-air until the bricklayers took him down. He only dislocated his leg and arm, and bruised his face, but the fiancé had a broken spine and his side was torn open.

The sister had convulsions. She lay on the ground tearing at the earth with her nails, raising a cloud of white dust. She wept for a long time, more than a month, and after that she grew thin and gaunt like her mother and her voice acquired the same cold, raw sound.

"You are my misfortune!" she would say.

The hunchback would stare down at the ground in silence. His sister took to wearing black, her brows were always knit, and on meeting her brother she clenched her teeth so violently that her cheek-bones stood out sharply. He did his best to avoid her and busied himself alone and silent over his drawings. They lived thus until he came of age and from that day on there was open war between them. Their entire lives were dedicated to this struggle which bound them together by the firm bonds of mutual insults and humiliations.

On the day he came of age he said to her in a tone of authority:

"There are no wise magicians or good fairies, there are only people. Some are bad, others are stupid, and all that is said about kindness is a fairy-tale! But I want that fairy-tale to come true. Do you remember what you said: in a rich house everyone must be either beautiful or clever? In a rich city too everything must be beautiful. I am buying a piece of land outside of town and I shall build a house there for myself and for other cripples like me. I shall take them away from this town where it is too painful for them to live and where they offend the sensibilities of people like you..."

"No," she said. "You will not do this! It is an insane idea!"

"It is your own idea."

They argued, coldly and rationally, as people do who hate each other and have no need to hide their hatred.

"It is decided," he said.

"Not by me," she answered.

He lifted his hump and went out, and soon afterward his sister learned that he had bought the land, and that the foundation was already being dug and carts were hauling up brick, stone, iron and wood.

"You still consider yourself a small boy?" she demanded. "Do you think this is a game?"

He did not reply.

Once a week his sister—straight-backed and proud—drove out of town in a small carriage drawn by a white horse which she drove herself, and driving slowly past the building site, coldly watched the meaty, red bricks being entwined with the tendons of the iron beams, and the yellow wood laid like nerve threads in the heavy mass. From the distance she saw her brother crawling crablike over the scaffolding, with his cane in his hand, a crumpled hat on his head, looking as dusty and grey as a spider. Later on, at home, she stared at his animated face and his dark eyes which had become softer and clearer than before.

"I tell you," he said, "this is a splendid idea of mine. It is good for us and for you too! It is a fine thing to build, and it seems to me that I shall soon be able to consider myself a happy man."

"Happy?" she echoed, measuring his deformed body with an enigmatical glance.

"Yes! Do you know, men who work are entirely different from us, they inspire one with strange thoughts. How fine it must be to be a bricklayer and to walk through the streets of the town in which he has built dozens of houses! There are a good many Socialists among the workers, they are sober-minded people and I must say they have a strong sense of dignity. Sometimes it seems to me that we know very little about our own people..."

"That is queer talk," she remarked.

The hunchback grew livelier and more talkative from day to day.

"As a matter of fact everything is proceeding as you wished it," he told her. "I shall be the wise magician who will rid our city of cripples. You could become the good fairy if you wished. Why do you not answer?"

"We shall speak of this later," she said, playing with her gold watch chain.

One day he addressed her in a language quite new to her:

"Perhaps I have wronged you even more than you me..."

She was astonished.

"I—wronged you!"

"Wait! I swear I am not so much to blame as you think! I am not very steady on my feet, perhaps I did push him that time, but I did not intend to, believe me! I am far more to blame for trying to disfigure the hand you struck me with..."

"Let us drop the subject," she said.

"We ought to be kinder to each other," the hunchback muttered. "I believe that kindness is not a dream, it is possible..."

The huge building outside of town grew with astonishing speed, it spread over the rich earth and rose to the sky that was always grey, always threatening rain.

One day a group of officials came to the site, they examined the building, talked quietly among themselves and ordered the work to stop.

"This is your doing!" cried the hunchback. He threw himself on his sister in his rage and seized her by the throat with his long, powerful hands. But people appeared from somewhere and tore him away from her.

"You see, gentlemen," she said to them, "he is

truly abnormal and needs a guardian! This began shortly after the death of our father whom he passionately loved. You may ask the servants, they all know of his illness. They have kept quiet about it, for they are good people who prize the honour of the house where many of them have lived from childhood. I too have concealed our misfortune, after all one cannot be proud of the fact that one's brother is insane..."

When he heard this his face turned blue and his eyes started out of their sockets. He lost the power of speech, and silently he clawed the people who were holding him, as she went on:

"Take this ruinous venture, the building of this house which I intend to turn over to the city for a psychiatric hospital to be named after my father..."

At this he uttered a loud cry and fainted. They carried him away.

His sister finished the building as speedily as he had begun it, and when the house was ready her brother was sent there as the first patient. He spent seven years there, quite enough time to become an imbecile. He developed melancholia. In the meantime his sister grew old, she lost all hope of ever being a mother and when at last she saw that her enemy was dead and would never revive she took him under her care.

And so they wander about the globe, moving from place to place like sightless birds, staring with dull, joyless eyes at everything and seeing nothing anywhere but themselves.

THE INTELLIGENTSIA

THE BLUE WATER seemed as thick as oil and the
ship's propeller turned softly and almost noiselessly
in it. The deck did not tremble underfoot, there was
only the straining and quivering of the mast pointing
up to the cloudless sky, and the soft humming of the
rigging, taut as violin strings, but one was too accustomed to that tremor to notice it and the ship seemed to
stand motionless, white and graceful as a swan on the
slippery water. To be conscious of motion one had to
look over the rail to where the green wave fell away
from the white ship's sides, crumpled up and disappeared

165

in broad soft folds, flashing a mercurial gleam and murmuring sleepily as it went.

It was early morning. The sea was not quite awake yet, the rosy hues of sunrise had not faded from the sky, but the wooded island of Gorgone was already passed, a grim lonely rock with a round grey tower on its summit and a huddle of small white houses on the shore of a sleepy bay. A few small boats had slipped swiftly by a short while back—sardine fishers from the island—leaving behind just a memory of the measured splash of long oars and the slender figures of the fisherman, standing in their boats, their bodies swaying as if bowing to the sun.

A wide strip of greenish foam trailed behind the ship and sea-gulls wheeled lazily over it. Now and again a water snake skimmed noiselessly over the surface of the water and dived suddenly swift as an arrow.

The purple mountains of the Ligurian coast rose dimly out of the sea in the distance; another two or three hours and the ship would enter the crowded harbour of Genoa, the city of marble.

Higher and higher rose the sun promising a sultry day.

Two stewards came running on deck: one was a young Neapolitan, slim and nimble, with an elusive expression on his mobile face; the other, a man of middle age, with a grey moustache and black eyebrows and a silvery bristle on his round skull, an aquiline nose and grave intelligent eyes. Laughing and cracking jokes, they quickly laid the table for coffee and hurried off. Presently one by one the passengers emerged from their cabins: a fat melancholy man with a small head and a flabby face, pink cheeks and puffy red lips that drooped wearily; a man wearing grey sideburns, tall and very well-groomed, with pale eyes and a small button nose on a flat sallow face. Behind him, stumbling on the brass-bound threshold, came a round ginger-haired man with a slight paunch and a military moustache, wearing an alpine costume and a hat with a green feather. All three went over to the ship's rail and the fat one, screwing up his eyes, said with a pensive air:

"Quiet, isn't it?"

The man with the sideburns thrust his hands into his pockets and set his feet apart so that he resembled an open scissors. The ginger-haired man took out a gold watch, as big as the pendulum of a grandfather's clock, glanced at it, then at the sky and along the deck and began to whistle, swinging the watch and tapping his foot.

Presently two ladies appeared—one young and plump with a china-doll face and mild, milky-blue eyes and dark eyebrows that seemed to be painted on, one slightly higher than the other; the other an older woman, with a sharp nose and faded hair fashionably arranged, a large black birth-mark on her left cheek, two gold chains hanging from her neck, a lorgnette and a bunch of trinkets at the waist of her grey gown.

Coffee was served. Without a word the young woman seated herself at the table and commenced to pour out the black liquid with a curiously rounded movement of her arms which were bare to the elbow. The men came over to the table and sat down. The fat one took a cup and said, with a sigh:

"It is going to be a hot day..."

"You are spilling your coffee on your lap," remarked the older woman.

Bending his head so that his jowls drooped and his chin pressed against his chest, he stood his cup on the table, brushed the drops of coffee from his grey trousers with his handkerchief and wiped his perspiring face.

"Yes," said the ginger-haired man, speaking suddenly in a loud voice and drawing up his short legs. "Yes, yes! If even the Leftists have begun to complain of hooliganism, that means..."

"Oh do stop chattering, Ivan!" the older woman interrupted him. "Is Lisa coming up?"

"She is not feeling well," replied the young woman in a deep voice.

"But the sea is perfectly calm..."

"Ach, when women are in such a delicate condition..."

The fat man smiled and closed his eyes languidly.

The man with the sideburns, who had been intently watching a school of dolphins gambolling on the smooth surface of the water, said:

"Dolphins are like pigs."

To which the ginger-haired man replied:

"In general there is much piggishness here."

The colourless lady raised her cup to her nose, smelt the coffee and made a grimace of distaste.

"Disgusting!"

"Yes, and as for the milk..." the fat man added, blinking in horror.

The lady with the china-doll face drawled: "Everything is filthy, filthy! And they look so disgustingly like Jews..."

The ginger-haired man was pouring out a long string of words into the ear of the man with the sideburns, as if he were rattling off a well-learnt lesson. The other listened with a sensuous curiosity, shaking his head slightly from side to side, his mouth a slit in his dry, flat face. Now and again he tried to interrupt, and began in a curious, fuzzy voice: "Now, in my own gubernia..."

But he went no further, and again bent his head attentively to the moustache of the ginger-haired man.

The fat man heaved a deep sigh and said:

"How you do buzz, Ivan..."

"Well, where is my coffee?"

He moved his chair noisily to the table, while his
companion remarked significantly:

"Ivan has ideas."

"You haven't had enough sleep," said the older woman, glancing at the Sideburns through her lorgnette.
He ran his hand over his face and looked at his
palm.

"I feel as if my face was powdered. Have you experienced the same sensation?"

"Yes, uncle!" cried the young lady. "It is the Italian
climate! It dries the skin dreadfully!"

"Have you noticed, Lydia, what awful sugar they
have," the older woman asked.

Just then a large man with thick grey curly hair,
a large nose, merry eyes and a cigar between his teeth
came on deck. The stewards standing by the rail bowed
respectfully to him.

"Good day, my lads, good day!" he said in a loud,
hoarse voice, nodding benevolently to them.

The Russians fell silent, glancing at him out of the
corner of their eyes, and the whiskered Ivan informed

the others in an undertone: "A retired soldier, one can tell at once..."

Conscious of their stares, the grey-haired man took the cigar from his mouth and bowed politely to the Russians. The older woman tossed her head, raised her lorgnette and fixed him with a challenging stare. The man with the moustache looked embarrassed for some reason, turned quickly away, pulled his watch from his pocket and began swinging it in the air again. Only the fat man replied to the bow, pressing his chin to his chest. This confused the Italian, who thrust his cigar back into the corner of his mouth and in a low voice asked the elderly steward:

"Russians?"

"Yes, sir! A Russian governor and his family..."

"What kind faces they always have..."

"Yes, a very good people..."

"The best of the Slavs certainly..."

"A trifle inconsiderate, I would say..."

"Inconsiderate? Really?"

"Yes, so it seems to me, inconsiderate of others."

The fat Russian reddened.

"They are talking about us," he said with a sheepish grin.

"What are they saying?" inquired the older woman, making a moue of distaste.

"They say we are the best of the Slavs," replied the fat man, giggling.

"They flatter us!" declared the woman, and the ginger-haired Ivan put away his watch and twirling his moustaches with both hands said disdainfully: "They are all amazingly ignorant about us..."

"There," said the fat one, "you are being praised and you declare it is out of ignorance..."

"Nonsense! I did not mean that, I meant in general... I know very well that we are the best."

The man with the sideburns, who had been closely watching the play of the dolphins all this time, sighed and shaking his head remarked: "What stupid fish!"

The grey-haired Italian was joined by two others, an old man wearing a black coat and glasses, and a long-haired, pale-faced youth with a tall forehead and thick eyebrows. All three stood at the rail a few yards away from the Russians.

"When I see Russians I always remember Messina," the grey-haired man said in a low voice.

"Remember the welcome we gave the Russian sailors who came to Naples?" said the young man.

"Yes! They will not forget that day in those forests of theirs!"

"Have you seen the medal that was struck in their honour?"

"Yes. I did not care for the workmanship!"

"They are talking about Messina," the fat man informed his companions.

"And they are laughing!" exclaimed the young woman. "Amazing!"

The gulls caught up with the boat. One of them hovered over the side, flapping its crooked wings violently. The young woman threw biscuits to it. The birds caught the morsels in their beaks, disappeared over the side of the boat and wheeled up again with loud cries into the blue emptiness over the sea. Coffee was brought to the Italians and they too began to feed the birds, throwing biscuits up into the air. The older woman frowned:

"Like monkeys!" she said in scorn.

The fat man listened to the lively conversation of the Italians and again reported: "He is not a soldier, but a merchant. He is talking about trading with us in grain. He says they could buy kerosene, timber and coal from us too."

"I could see at once that he was not a soldier," the older woman declared.

The ginger-haired man resumed his whispered discourse with Sideburns, who listened with his mouth drooping sceptically, while the young Italian, glancing now and again toward the Russians, was saying:

173

"What a pity we know so little of that land of huge people with light-blue eyes."

The sun was already high up and the heat was intense. The sea shone with dazzling brightness and in the distance the contours of mountains or clouds rose out of the sea.

"Annette," said Sideburns, his mouth stretched to his ears in a broad smile, "just listen to this absurd Jean, he has thought of a remarkably clever way of getting rid of those rebels in the villages!"

Rocking back and forth in his chair, he began to speak slowly in a flat voice as if translating from a foreign language:

"He says that at village fairs and on holidays the local land authorities should prepare a large quantity of stakes and stones at the expense of the Treasury and then present the muzhiks, also at the Treasury's expense, with ten, twenty or fifty pails of vodka, depending on the number of people. That will do the trick!"

"I do not understand," said the older woman. "Is it a joke?"

"No, quite seriously," the ginger-haired man hastened to assure her. "Just think of it, ma tante..."

The young woman opened her eyes wide and shrugged her shoulders.

"What nonsense! To let them swill vodka at the expense of the Treasury, when as it is..."

"No, wait, Lydia!" cried the ginger-haired man, springing up on his chair. The man with the sideburns laughed noiselessly, his mouth wide open and swaying from side to side.

"Think of it—the hooligans who don't drink themselves senseless will beat one another up with the stakes and the stones. You see?"

"Why one another?" inquired the fat man.

"But you are joking?" the older woman insisted.

The ginger-haired man, spreading out his short arms, went on excitedly: "Whenever the authorities suppress them, the Leftists start shouting about brutalities and atrocities, so we must find a way of getting them to suppress themselves. Right?"

The boat rolled suddenly. The plump woman caught at the table in fright, the dishes rattled, and the older woman clutched at the fat man's shoulder. "What was that?" she cried sternly.

"We are turning round..."

The coastline grew more and more distinct: hills and misty mountains covered with gardens; blue rocks amid the vineyards, white houses peeping out of dense green shrubbery, window-panes gleaming in the sunlight. Bright patches of colour already stood out—at the very water's edge a small house nestled among the rocks facing the sea, its façade covered with a thick mass of bright purple flowers and with scarlet geraniums pouring in rich profusion from the stone terrace above. The gay colours made the shore look warm and inviting and the soft contours of the mountains seemed to beckon one into the cool shade of the gardens.

"How crowded everything is here," remarked the fat man with a sigh. The older woman glanced at him coldly, then raising her lorgnette she studied the shore, pursing her thin lips and tossing her head.

There were now many dark-complexioned men in light suits on the deck, conversing in loud tones. The Russian ladies looked at them with haughty disdain like queens at their subjects.

"How they do gesticulate," remarked the young woman. The fat man explained:

"That is a peculiarity of the language, it is so poor that it must be accompanied by gestures..."

"Good heavens!" said the older woman with a deep sigh, then after a brief pause, asked:

"Are there many museums in Genoa as well?"

"Only three, I believe," replied the fat man.

"And that cemetery?" asked the young woman.

"Yes, the campo santo. And the churches of course."

"And I suppose the cabs are as wretched as in Naples?"

The ginger-haired man and the man with the side-burns got up and walked over to the railing carrying on an earnest conversation, both talking at once.

"What is that Italian saying?" the lady asked, patting her elegant coiffure. She had sharp elbows and large yellow ears that resembled faded leaves. The fat man obediently listened intently to the lively talk of the curly-haired Italian.

"They have what must be a very ancient law, signori, forbidding Jews to visit Moscow—that is evidently a survival of depotism, Ivan the Terrible, you know! Even in England there are many archaic laws which remain in force to this day. But perhaps this particular Jew was deceiving me, at any rate he for some reason had no right to visit Moscow—the ancient city of the tsars, a holy city..."

"And here in Rome—which is far older and holier than Moscow—the mayor is a Jew," said the youth, with a laugh.

"And how cleverly he outwits the tailor Pope!*" interjected an old man in spectacles clapping his hands.

"What is that old man shouting about?" the lady asked lowering her lorgnette.

"Some nonsense. They are speaking in the Neapolitan dialect."

---

*A play of words—the Pope's name was Sarto meaning "tailor." — *Tr.*

"...He went to Moscow, and since one must have a roof over one's head this Jew went to a prostitute, signori. He had nowhere else to go, he said."

"A cock-and-bull story!" declared the old man firmly, waving the story-teller away.

"To say the truth I think so myself."

"Well, what happened then?" the youth asked.

"She turned him over to the police, but first the took money from him, as from an ordinary customer..."

"How vile!" said the old man. "That man had a filthy imagination, that's all. I knew some Russians at the University, they were very fine fellows..."

The fat Russian, dabbing his perspiring face with his handkerchief, said to the ladies in a lazy drawl:

"He is telling a Jewish anecdote."

"With such animation!" laughed the young woman, and the other remarked: "You know, these people with their gestures and their noise are somehow terribly boring."

On shore the town was growing before their eyes: houses came into view from behind hills, the gaps between them growing less and less until they formed a solid wall of buildings that seemed in the sunlight to be carved out of ivory.

"It looks like Yalta," said the young woman rising to her feet. "I shall go down to Lisa."

178

She sailed across the deck, her large body draped in light-blue cloth swaying slightly as she walked, and when she passed the group of Italians, the grey-haired man stopped speaking to remark in an undertone:

"What beautiful eyes!"

"Yes," said the old man in the spectacles, shaking his head. "Basilida must have looked like that!"

"But Basilida was a Byzantine, was she not?"

"I see her as a Slav."

"They are speaking of Lydia," said the stout man.

"What are they saying?" asked the woman. "Something insulting, no doubt?"

"No, about her eyes. They admire them..."

The woman made a face.

The steamer, its brasswork glittering, edged in swiftly and gently to the shore. Behind the dark walls of the pier rose a forest of masts. Here and there bright shreds of flags hung motionless. The black smoke melted in the air and the smell of oil and coal dust, harbour noises and the muffled roar of a big city reached the boat.

The stout man suddenly laughed aloud.

"What is the joke?" the lady asked, narrowing her faded grey eyes.

"The Germans will smash them, by God! You will see!"

"But why should that make you so happy?"

"Oh, I don't know..."

The man with the sideburns, looking down at his feet, asked the ginger-haired man in a loud, meticulous voice: "Would that be a pleasant surprise for you or not?"

The other twirled his moustaches fiercely but made no reply.

The steamer slowed down. The murky green water which reflected nothing of the marble buildings, the tall towers, or the grillwork balconies, slapped itself shudderingly against the ship's sides as if in complaint. The black maw of the port packed tight with vessels of all kinds opened wide to receive them.

THE TROUBLE-MAKER

A MAN IN A LIGHT suit, lean and clean-shaven like an American, sat down at an iron table near the door of the restaurant and called out in a lazy drawl:

"Ga-aarçon..."

Acacia blossoms hung in thick white profusion all around and the golden sunbeams filled earth and sky with the gentle gladness of springtide. Little shaggy-eared donkeys tripped down the street with a pattering of hoofs, heavy draught horses jogged along, the people too walked at a leisurely pace, and it was clear that every living creature wished to linger as long as possible in the sunshine and breathe the air heavy with the sweet scent of flowers.

Children, the heralds of spring, flashed by, the sun tinting their clothes with bright hues; gaily dressed women, who belong to a sunny day as the stars belong to the night, sailed along, swaying slightly as they walked.

The man in the light suit had a curiously scrubbed look about him: as if he had been extremely dirty and had just been washed clean, but so vigorously that all vividness had been rubbed off him for ever. He looked around him with his faded eyes as if he were counting the sun spots on the walls of the houses and on everything that moved along the dark street and over the broad flagstones of the boulevard. His flaccid lips were pursed and he was softly whistling a queer, sad tune, and drumming his long white fingers on the edge of the table. His nails gleamed palely and in his other hand he held a tan glove with which he beat time on his knee. He had the face of a man of intelligence and resolution, it seemed a pity that all warmth had been so roughly wiped off that face.

As the waiter, with a deferential bow, placed before him a cup of coffee, a small bottle of green liqueur and some biscuits, a man sat down at the next table. He was a powerfully built man with agate eyes; his cheeks, neck and hands were smoke-begrimed and his burly frame had such steel-like quality of strength that he seemed part of some huge machine.

When the eyes of the clean man rested wearily on him, he raised himself slightly, touched his cap with his fingers and said through his thick moustache:

"Good day, Mr. Engineer."

"Ah, you again, Trama!"

"Yes, it's me, Mr. Engineer..."

"Well, we may expect something, eh?"

"How is your work getting on?"

"You can't make conversation with questions alone, my friend," said the engineer with a faint smile on his thin lips.

His companion pushed his hat on to one ear and laughed heartily.

"Right you are!" he said through his laughter, "but I swear I'd give a lot to know..."

A rough-haired, piebald donkey drawing a coal cart stopped in his tracks, stretched out his neck and emitted a mournful cry, but evidently the sound of his own voice did not please him that day, for he broke off in confusion on a high note, shook his shaggy ears and, lowering his head, trotted on with a clatter of hoofs.

"I'm waiting for that machine of yours as impatiently as I would wait for a new book to draw new wisdom from."

"I do not quite understand the analogy," murmured the engineer sipping his coffee.

"Don't you agree that a machine frees man's physical energy as much as a good book frees his spirit?"

"Ah!" said the engineer, raising his head, "perhaps you're right." "And now, I suppose, you will start your propaganda?" he added, placing the empty cup back on the table.

"I have started already..."

"Strikes and disturbances again, eh?"

The other shrugged his shoulders, smiling gently.

"If only all that were unnecessary..."

An old woman in black, as austere as a nun, silently proffered a bunch of violets to the engineer. He took two and handing one to his companion, said reflectively:

"You have such a good head, Trama, it is a pity you are an idealist..."

"Thank you for the flowers and the compliment. A pity, you say?"

"Yes! You are essentially a poet, and you could learn to become a good engineer if you tried."

Trama chuckled, his white teeth gleaming.

"Ah, there you're right!" he said. "An engineer is a poet. Working with you I have learned that..."

"You are very kind..."

"I have thought, why should Monsieur the Engineer not become a Socialist? A Socialist must be a poet too..."

They both laughed in complete understanding, these two men so strikingly different in appearance, the one dry, nervous, with the rubbed-out features and faded eyes, and the other looking as if he had been hammered out in a forge shop only yesterday and had not yet been polished.

"No, Trama, I would prefer to have my own workshop and some three dozen good lads like yourself working for me. Then we would be able to do something..."

He tapped the table lightly with his fingers and sighed as he put the violets in his buttonhole.

"Devil take it," cried Trama growing excited, "to think that trifles can prevent a man from living and working..."

"Oh so you call human history a trifle, master mechanic Trama?" queried the engineer with a faint smile. The worker snatched off his hat, gesturing with it as he went on heatedly:

"Ah, what is the history of my ancestors?"

"*Your* ancestors?" queried the engineer, accentuating the first word with a more caustic smile.

"Yes, mine! Insolence du think? Perhaps. But why are Giordano Bruno, Vico and Mazzini not my ancestors? Am I not living in their world, am I not enjoying the fruit of their great minds?"

"Oh, in that sense!"

"Everything the departed have given to the world is mine!"

"Of course," said the engineer, knitting his brows gravely.

"And everything that has been done before me, before us, is the ore which we must turn into steel, is it not?"

"Why, of course, that is obvious!"

"After all, you educated men, just as we workers, are reaping the fruit of the minds of the past."

"I do not deny that," said the engineer, looking down to discover a small, ragged boy like a much-battered ball, standing beside him holding a bunch of crocuses in his filthy little paws and urging insistently:

"Buy my flowers, signor..."

"I have some..."

"You can never have too many flowers..."

"Right you are, lad," said Trama, "Bravo, give me two..."

And when the boy had given him the flowers he raised his hat and offered a bunch to the engineer.

"Thank you."

"It's a glorious day, isn't it?"

"Yes, even at fifty I can appreciate its beauty..."

The engineer glanced thoughtfully about him with narrowed eyes and heaved a sigh.

"I daresay you feel the warmth of the spring sun coursing in your veins so keenly, not only because you are young, but because I believe the whole world looks different to you than it does to me. Is that not so?"

"I do not know," replied the other laughing. "But life is good!"

"Because of what it promises?" the engineer asked sceptically. The question appeared to sting his companion, for replacing his cap on his head, he answered impulsively:

"Life is good because of all that I love in it! Damn it all, my friend, words to me are not merely sounds and letters; when I read a book, look at a picture or behold something beautiful I feel as if I had created it all with my own hands!"

They both laughed at that, the one frankly and heartily as though proud of his ability to laugh well, throwing his head back and thrusting out his broad chest, the other, almost soundlessly, chokingly, exposing his teeth with their gold fillings that looked as if he had recently been chewing gold and had forgotten to clean it off his teeth.

"You're a good lad, Trama, it is always a pleasure to see you," said the engineer and added with a wink: "If only you weren't such a troubly-maker..."

"Oh, I'm always making trouble..."

And screwing up his fathomless black eyes in an expression of mock gravity, he inquired:

"I trust our behaviour was quite correct that time?"

The engineer shrugged his shoulders and rose.

"Oh yes, quite. That affair cost the firm some thirty-seven thousand lire, you know..."

"It might have been wiser to have added that to the men's wages..."

"H'm! You're wrong. Wiser, you say? Every beast has his own brand of wisdom."

He held out a dry yellow hand and when the worker shook it, said:

"I still think you ought to study and study hard..."

"I learn something every minute..."

"You would make an engineer with a rich imagination."

"Oh, my imagination comes in quite handy as it is!"

"Well, so long, my stubborn friend!"

The engineer walked off under the acacias, through the tracery of sunbeams, taking long strides with his lanky legs and pulling his glove on to the thin long fingers of his right hand. The little dark waiter moved away from the door of the restaurant where he had been listening to the conversation and said to the worker who was rummaging in his purse for some coppers:

"Getting old, our engineer..."

"Oh, he can still hold his own!" exclaimed the worker

confidently. "There's plenty of fire under that skull of his..."

"Where will you be speaking next time?"

"In the same place, the labour exchange. Have you heard me?"

"Three times, comrade..."

Shaking hands warmly they parted with a smile; the one walking off in the opposite direction from that the engineer had taken, the other humming pensively as he commenced to clear the tables.

A group of school children in white aprons, boys and girls, marched by in the middle of the road, scattering noise and laughter all around them; the pair in the lead blew lustily into paper trumpets, and the acacias softly showered them with snowy petals.

Always, and especially in springtime, the sight of children prompts one to call after them loudly and gaily:

"Hey, there, young folk! May the future be yours!"

VENDETTA

WHEN MAN CAN no longer find a crust of bread on the earth that has been enriched by the bones of his ancestors; if, driven by need, he is forced to leave his native soil and go to South America, thirty day's journey from home—if things come to such a pass, what can one expect a man to do?

It does not matter who he is—he is like a child torn from its mother's breast. The wine of a foreign land tastes bitter to him; instead of gladdening his heart it fills him with longing, makes him listless

191

and flabby as a sponge, and his heart, torn out of the homeland's breast, absorbs all manner of evil and wickedness as a sponge absorbs water.

In Calabria our young men usually marry before leaving home to cross the ocean, believing, perhaps, that their love for a woman might deepen their love for their country—for a woman holds the same attraction for a man as his country, and nothing can protect a man better in a strange land than true love that calls him back to his native soil, to his loved one's breast.

But these marriages, overshadowed by poverty and separation, are nearly always the prologues to grim dramas of fate, vengeance and bloodshed, as was the case not long ago in Senerchia, a community situated in the Appenine Mountains.

It is a simple and terrible story which might have been taken from the Bible, and to begin at the beginning we must go back five years. Five years ago a handsome young woman named Emilia Bracco lived in the little village of Saracena high up in the mountains. Her husband had gone to America and she lived with his parents. She was a strong, healthy girl and an able worker, endowed with a fine voice and a merry nature, fond of joke and apt to flaunt her beauty a little, exciting the passions of the village lads and the woodsmen from the hills. With skilful banter she guarded her honour, and though her gay laughter stirred many fond hopes, no man could ever boast of having won her.

Now, no one in the world suffers the pangs of envy so much as the Devil and an old woman. Emilia lived with her mother-in-law and the Devil is always to be found where there is evil work to be done.

"You are too gay without your husband, my dear," the old woman would say. "I think I shall write to him about it. Take care, I am watching every step you take. Remember, your honour is our honour..."

At first Emilia calmly assured her mother-in-law that she loved her husband, and had no cause to reproach herself. But the old woman continued to insult her with her ugly suspicions, and egged on by the devil, began to spread the rumour that her daughter-in-law had lost all shame.

When she heard this, Emilia was frightened and she implored the old witch not to ruin her by her malicious gossip, swearing that she had never been faithless to her husband, that even in her dreams she had never been tempted to deceive him. But the old woman would not believe her.

"I know how much such vows are worth," she scoffed. "Was I not young myself once? No, I have already written to him to come back at once and avenge his honour!"

"You have written to him ?" Emilia gasped in horror.

"I have."

"Very well…"

Our men are as jealous as Arabs, and Emilia knew what awaited her on her husband's return.

The next day, when the mother-in-law went to the forest to gather dry brushwood, Emilia followed her with an axe hidden beneath her skirts. Later on, she went to the carabinieri and told them that she had killed her mother-in-law.

"It is better to be a murderess than to be looked upon as a harlot when one is innocent," she said.

Her trial was a triumph for her. Nearly the entire population of Senerchia went to testify on her behalf and many pleaded with the judge with tears in their eyes, saying: "She is innocent, her life has been ruined unjustly."

Only His Eminence, the Archbishop Cozzi, dared to raise his voice against the unfortunate woman. He refused to believe in her innocence.

He spoke of the need to uphold the ancient traditions, and he warned the people that they were making the same mistake as had the Greeks when they acquitted Phryne, allowing her beauty to blind them to her unseemly conduct. He said everything he had to say and perhaps it was thanks to him that Emilia was sentenced to four years' imprisonment.

Like Emilia's husband, his fellow-villager Donato Guarnaccia had also gone across the ocean, leaving his young wife behind at home to the melancholy task of Penelope—to weave dreams of life without living.

Three years ago Donato received a letter from his mother informing him that his wife Theresa had given herself to his father—her husband—and was living with him. The old woman and the Devil again, you see!

Guarnaccia bought a ticket for the first steamer bound for Naples and turned up unexpectedly at his home as if he had dropped from the skies.

His wife and his father feigned astonishment, and he, being a hard-headed, suspicious lad, kept his counsel at first, wishing to verify the truth of the report, for he had heard Emilia Bracco's story. He treated his wife tenderly and for a time both seemed to enjoy a second honeymoon, a passionate feast of youth.

His mother tried to pour poison into his ear, but he stopped her: "Enough!" he said. "I shall judge for myself. Let me be."

He knew that one who has been wronged cannot be believed, be it one's own mother.

Nearly half the summer passed thus in peace and tranquillity and they might have lived thus to the end of their days, if the father had not taken advantage of the son's brief absences from home to renew his attentions to his daughter-in-law. But now she resisted the advances of the old lecher and this angered him—he could not endure to be so suddenly deprived of the enjoyment of her young body. And he resolved to take revenge on her.

"You shall perish," he threatened her.

"So shall you," she retorted.

We are a people of few words.

The next day he said to his son: "Do you know that your wife has been unfaithful to you?"

The son grew pale, and looking his father straight in the eye, he asked: "What proof have you?"

"Those who have enjoyed her caresses have told me that she has a large birth-mark in the lower part of her belly—is that so?"

"Very well," said Donato. "Since you, my father, tell me that she is guilty she shall die!"

The shameless father nodded his head.

"Of course! Loose women must be killed."

"And men too," said Donato and went away.

He went to his wife, laid his heavy hands on her shoulders.

"Listen to me. I know you have been unfaithful to me. For the sake of the love we bore each other before and after your betrayal, tell me who is the man?"

"Your accursed father alone could have told you! He alone..." she cried.

"It is he, then?" demanded the peasant, the blood rushing to his eyes.

"He took me by force, with threats. But hear the whole truth..."

She paused, struggling for breath.

"Speak!" cried her husband shaking her.

"Yes, yes," she whispered in despair. "We lay together he and I, as man and wife, some thirty, forty times..."

Donato rushed into the house, seized his gun and ran out to the field whither his father had gone and there he said all that men say to each other at such moments, and with two shots he finished him. Then he spat on the body and smashed the skull with his rifle butt. They say that he made mockery of the body for a long time, that he jumped on its back and danced a dance of vengeance upon it.

Then he went to his wife and loading his shotgun, said: "Stand back four paces and say your prayers..."

She began to weep and beg him to spare her life.

"No," he said. "I must do as justice demands, as you would have done had I wronged you..."

And he shot her dead as he would have shot a bird, and gave himself up to the authorities. And as he passed down the village street, the people made way for him and many of them said: "You have behaved as a man of honour, Donato..."

At the trial he defended himself with grim energy, with all the crude eloquence of a primitive soul.

"I take a woman in order that the fruit of our love shall be a child in whom both of us, she and I, should live! When a man loves, neither father nor mother exists for him, only love exists. May love be eternal and those who defile it, man or woman, be they cursed with sterility, with fearful pestilence and agonizing death..."

The counsel for the defence demanded that the jury return a verdict of murder in a fit of rage, but the jury acquitted Donato amid stormy applause from the public. And Donato returned to Senerchia like a conquering hero. He was hailed as a man who had adhered stringently to the old national traditions of bloody vengeance for besmirched honour.

Shortly after Donato's acquittal, Emilia Bracco was released from jail. It was winter, the season when Nature mourns. The feast of the Birth of Christ was approaching, a time when men desire above all things to be among their own kin, around their own warm hearth. But Emilia and Donato were alone, for theirs was not the fame that evoked the respect of their fellowmen—a murderer remains a murderer after all. He may shock people, he may be vindicated, but how can he be loved? Both of them had blood on their hands and broken hearts; both had suffered the painful drama of trial, and it was no surprise to anyone in Senerchia that these two people, branded by Fate, should be drawn together and seek to brighten each other's broken lives, for they were both young and they both yearned for tenderness.

"What shall we do here amid all these painful memories of the past?" Donato said to Emilia after their first kisses.

"If my husband returns he will kill me, for now I have truly been faithless to him in thought," said Emilia.

They decided to go overseas as soon as they had saved enough money for the journey, and perhaps they would have succeeded in finding a little happiness and a peaceful haven for themselves. But they lived among people who reasoned in this wise:

"We can forgive a murder of passion. We applauded crime committed to defend honour. But are these two not trampling the very traditions in whose name so much blood was spilt?"

These harsh and sinister judgements, echoes of the

grim and hoary past, sounded ever louder until finally they reached the ears of Emilia's mother, Serafina Amato, a strong, proud woman, who in spite of her fifty years still possessed the beauty of one born in the mountains.

At first she did not believe the insulting rumours. "Slander," she said. "Have you forgotten how my daughter suffered to protect her honour."

"No, it is she who has forgotten," people replied.

Whereupon Serafina, who lived in another village, came to her daughter and said:

"People are beginning to talk about you, I do not want to hear these things said of you. What you did in the past was the action of a pure and honourable woman in spite of the bloodshed, and so it must remain as a lesson to all men!"

Her daughter began to weep.

"The world exists for man, but what is man if he cannot exist for himself?"

"Ask the priest if you are stupid enough not to know the answer yourself," her mother replied.

Then she went to Donato and issued him a stern warning.

"Leave my daughter alone, or you shall live to rue it!"

"Listen," the young man implored her. "I love your

daughter with all my heart. She is as unfortunate as I am. Permit me to take her away with me to another land and all will be well!"

But he only poured oil on the flames.

"You want to run away?" cried Serafina in fury and despair. "No, that shall never be!"

They parted snarling like beasts and staring at each other with hatred in their eyes.

From that day Serafina began to stalk the lovers as a clever dog stalks game. But this did not prevent them from meeting secretly at night—for love too is as cunning and clever as a beast.

But once Serafina overheard her daughter and Guarnacchia discussing a plan of escape—and in that evil moment she resolved on a monstrous deed.

On Sunday the people gathered in the church to hear Mass. In front stood the women in gaudy holiday skirts and shawls, and behind them knelt the men. Our lovers too came to pray to the Madonna to help them.

Serafina Amato entered the church later than the others. She too was dressed in her holiday clothes, and in the folds of the wide embroidered apron which she wore over her skirt, she had hidden an axe.

Slowly, with a prayer on her lips, she crept over to the image of Archangel Michael, the patron saint of Senerchia, knelt down before him, touched his hand with her palm and her lips and, creeping stealthily up to her daughter's seducer who stood on his knees with the others, struck him twice on the head cutting a Roman figure V, the sign of the vendetta on his skull.

A wave of horror seized the congregation. They rushed shouting and screaming to the exit. Many fell senseless on the tiled floor, many wept like children. But Serafina stood with the axe poised over poor Donato and her senseless daughter like some village Nemesis.

She stood thus for many minutes and when the people recovered from the shock and seized her, she commenced to pray loudly, raising her eyes burning with savage joy to the heavens:

"Saint Michael, I give thanks to you! It is you who gave me the strength to avenge my daughter's honour!"

When she learned that Guarnachia was still alive and had been carried to the apothecary, where his frightful wounds were being dressed, she was seized with a fit of trembling, and rolling her mad, horror-filled eyes, she said:

"No, no, I believe in God. That man will die. I struck him two fatal wounds, my hands felt it, and— God is just—that man must die!"

The woman will soon stand trial and of course she will be severely punished, but what can any punishment teach to a person who believes that he has the right to inflict violence on others? Does iron become softer for being hammered?

The judge of men says to the accused: you are guilty. The accused replies: guilty or not guilty, all remains as before.

And in the final end, dear signori, it must be said that a man must grow and have increase where the Lord has placed him, where he is loved by the soil and by a woman...

GIOVANNI TUBA

FROM EARLY CHILDHOOD Old Giovanni Tuba lost his heart to the sea, that blue expanse now gentle and serene like the glance of a young girl, now stormy like the passionate heart of a woman; that wilderness that absorbs the sunshine the fish have no need of, and which brings forth nothing from contact with the golden sunbeams other than beauty and dazzling brilliance; the treacherous sea with its eternal song that fills one with an irresistible desire to sail away into its distances. Many of man has it lured away from the dumb, stony earth which demands so much moisture from the skies, so much toil from man and gives so little joy in return!

Even as a boy working in a vineyard that clung to the mountain side in terraces held up by grey stone walls; amid the spreading fig-trees and olives with their leaves of beaten metal, the dark green orange-trees and the tangled branches of pomegranates, under the bright sun on the hot earth amid the scent of flowers, even then Tuba gazed hungrily at the blue sea with the eyes of one under whose feet the earth pitched and rolled. He gazed, drinking in the salty air until he was drunk with it, becoming absent-minded, indolent and disobedient as is always the case with those who fall under the sea's spell, who fall head over heels in love with the sea...

And on holidays, early in the morning, when the sun had barely risen and the sky over Sorrento was still pink as though woven from apricot blossoms, young Tuba, as shaggy as a sheep dog, would go scampering down the hillside his fishing rod over his shoulder, leaping from rock to rock, a veritable boneless bundle of springy muscles, and run down to the sea, his broad freckled face lit up by a happy smile as the sharp tang of the sea, stronger than the sweet fragrance of the awakening flowers, floated toward him on the fresh morning air, and he heard the low murmur of the waves as they rippled over stones down below, drawing him toward them like maidens...

There he is perched on the edge of a pinkish-grey rock, his bronze legs dangling, his huge black eyes like two plums probing the transparent greenish water whose liquid glass reveals to him a wondrous world far more entrancing than all the fairy-tales he has ever heard: red-gold seaweed at the sea's bottom waving among stones covered with carpets; gaily-hued "violi," the flowers of the sea, floating out of a forest of seaweed, "perche," with the bleary eyes of drunkards, striped noses and blue spots on their bellies; golden "sarpe," the impudent striped "canie," black "guarracini," darting swiftly about like merry devils, "sparaglioni" and "occhiate" shining like silver saucers and a host of other lovely fish—all of them cunning creatures who peck at the bait with their tiny teeth before snatching it with their round little mouths.

In this bright, placid water bewhiskered shrimps float like birds in the air; hermit crabs crawl over the stones at the bottom dragging their ornamented shell-homes behind them; starfish, red as blood, propel themselves gently forward; purple medusas rock silently, and now and again the evil head of the sharp-toothed muraena thrusts itself out from beneath a stone, its red speckled snaky body writhing this way and that—just like the witch in the fairy-tale, but much more frightening and ugly; and suddenly a grey octopus spreads itself out in the water like a dirty rag, and dashes hurriedly off after some prey; and now a lobster comes along its whiskers as long as bamboo fishing rods twitching as it goes; these and a host of other wondrous creatures dwell in this transparent water under a sky as clear but far emptier than the sea.

And the sea breathes, its blue bosom rising and falling. Green white-tipped waves break against the rock on which Tuba sits chasing one another merrily in an effort to lick his feet—sometimes they succeed, making him start and smile, and then they laugh gaily and run away from the rock as if in fear, only to come rippling up to it again. A sunbeam penetrates deep into the water, making a funnel of bright light thrust into the bosom of the water. His soul slumbers blissfully, undisturbed by thoughts or desires, content to feast in silence on what it sees; bright waves ripple over his whole being, and his soul is as boundlessly free as the sea itself.

That was how he spent his holidays, and after a time the sea began to call to him on weekdays as well, for when once it has taken possession of a man's heart he becomes a part of it, just as the heart is only part of the man. And so he left his plot of land to his brother and went off with a company of other men, in love with the sea like himself, to the shores of Sicily to fish for coral. Fine work, but dangerous too, for a man can drown ten times a day. But what wonderful things he sees when the net rises heavily out of the blue water—a semi-circular net rimmed with iron teeth seething like thoughts in the brain with all forms of life and colour, and in the middle, the pink branches of the precious corals, the sea's gift to man!

And so this man over whom the sea had cast its spell was lost for ever to the land. Women too he loved as if in a dream, briefly and silently, for he could speak to them only of that which he knew—of fish and corals, of the play of the waves, the caprices of the wind and of big ships which sail unknown seas. He was timid on land, he walked the earth cautiously, suspiciously, and he was silent with people, gazing at them searchingly with the keen eye of one accustomed to plumbing the treacherous deeps and not trusting them. But on sea he was quietly happy, attentive to his comrades and as agile as a dolphin.

But however good the life a man chooses for himself, it never lasts more than a few score years. When the old salt reached the age of eighty his hands, twisted by rheumatism, refused to work—enough!—his knotted legs barely supported his bowed body, and, now an old weather-beaten man, Tuba sorrowfully landed on the island, climbed the hill to his brother's cabin, to join his brother's children and grandchildren, folk too poor to be kind now that Tuba could no longer bring them quantities of delicious fish as of old.

The old man was miserable among these people, they watched too carefully the bits of bread he thrust with his crooked old hand into his toothless mouth. He soon saw that he was one too many among them. His soul grew dark, his heart contracted with pain, the wrinkles on his sun-dried skin deepened and a new ache racked his old bones. All day long from morning till night he would sit on the stones by the door of the cabin, his old eyes staring out at the bright sea where his life had melted away, the blue sea sparkling in the sunshine as beautiful as a dream.

It was far away from him, and the journey down to the sea shore was not easy for an old man. But he made up his mind, and one quiet night he set out down the hillside, crawling over the sharp stones like a crushed lizard, and when he reached the waves— they met him with their familiar murmuring splash against the earth's dead stones, a sound far more gentle than the voices of men—the old man, as people afterwards guessed, fell upon his knees, looked up at the sky, prayed a little for all men who were strangers to him, then cast aside the rags that covered his old bones, laid that old skin—his own yet not his own—on the rocks, and walked into the water. Tossing his hoary head, he lay down on his back, his face upturned to the sky, and swam off into the distance, to where the dark blue of the sky touches the waves with the edge of its purple 'mantle, and the stars are so close to the water that it seems one can reach them by stretching out one's hand.

On soft summer nights the sea is as calm as the soul of a child wearied by the day's play; it sleeps, sighing faintly and doubtless dreaming bright dreams; if you swim by night through the thick warm water blue sparks flash beneath your hands, a blue flame spreads about you, and your soul melts softly in a gentle radiance as caressing as a tale told by a mother.

OLD CECCO

The sun rises amid a hallowed silence, and a bluish mist, heavy with the sweet scent of the golden furze, floats skyward from the rocky island.

Standing in the midst of the dark mass of sleepy water under the pale cupola of the sky, the island is like an altar to the Sun God.

The stars have just faded, but white Venus still shines alone in the chill vastness of the dim sky above a delicate ridge of fluffy clouds. The clouds are tinged faintly with pink and glow softly in the light of the first beam, and their reflection on the tranquil bosom of the sea is like mother-o'-pearl that has risen to the surface from the blue deeps.

The blades of grass and the petals of the flowers laden with silvery dew reach out toward the sun. The shining drops of dew hanging at the tips of the stalks swell up and fall to the ground which has perspired in its sleep. One waits to hear the soft tinkling sound of their fall, and grieves when he fails to hear it.

The birds are up and flitting about among the olive leaves singing their morning song, and from below come the heavy sighs of the sea awakened by the sun.

Nevertheless it is quiet, for the people are still asleep. In the freshness of early morning the scent of the flowers and grasses is stronger than sound.

From the doorway of a little white house so overgrown with vines that it looks like a boat lashed by green waves, old Ettore Cecco comes out to meet the sun. A lonely little old man, with the long arms of a monkey, the bare skull of a sage, and a face so furrowed by time that his eyes are almost completely hidden in the wrinkled skin.

Raising his black hairy hand slowly to his forehead he looks up at the pink sky and surveys the scene around him: the rich gamut of emerald and gold, the rose, yellow and red of the blooms against the greyish-purple of the rocks. His dark face quivers in a gentle smile, and he nods his round, heavy head in approval.

He stands as though supporting some heavy weight, his back slightly bent, his legs wide apart, and around him the young day glows and sparkles, brighter shines the green of the vines, louder sounds the twittering of the gold finches; the quails flutter among the blackberry and spurge thickets, and somewhere a blackbird, as jaunty and carefree as a Neapolitan, whistles a merry note.

Old Cecco raises his long weary arms above his head and stretches himself as if about to fly down into the sea which is as calm as wine in a chalice.

Having stretched his old bones, he lowers himself on to a boulder beside the door, takes a postcard out of his jacket pocket, holds it away from him and gazes long at it with narrowed eyes, his lips moving soundlessly. His large face with its silvery bristle lights up in a new smile, a smile in which love, sorrow and pride are strangely mingled.

Before him on the slip of pasteboard is a drawing in blue ink of two strapping lads, seated side by side and smiling gaily, two young men with curly hair and large heads like Old Cecco's. On top of the card in large clear type are the printed words:

"Arturo and Enrico Cecco, two noble champions of the interests of their class. They organized 25,000 textile workers who earned 6 dollars a week, and for this they were thrown into prison.

"Long live the fighters for social justice!"

Old Cecco cannot read, moreover the caption is printed in a foreign language, but he knows what it says, every word is familiar to him, every word is like a trumpet blast.

This blue postcard has brought the old man much trouble and anxiety. He received it two months ago and his paternal instinct told him at once that something was amiss: the portraits of poor men are printed only when they break the law.

Cecco hid the slip of paper in his pocket, but it was like a heavy weight against his heart and it grew heavier from day to day. More than once he was about to show it to the priest, but long experience had taught him that people are right when they say: "A priest may speak the truth to God about Man, but never the truth to Man!"

The first person he asked to explain the mysterious significance of the postcard was a red-haired artist, a long, lanky foreigner, who often came to Cecco's house. He would set up his easel at a convenient angle and then lie down to sleep beside it, with his head in the square shadow cast by the unfinished painting.

"Signor," Cecco asked him, "what have these men done?"

The artist glanced at the smiling faces of the old man's sons and said: "Something jolly most likely."

"But what is written here about them?"

"It is in English. Besides the English, no one understands their language except God, and my wife too, if she is telling the truth in this case. It most cases she doesn't . . ."

The artist chattered like a magpie; he was evidently incapable of taking anything seriously and the old man went away in disgust. The following day he went to the stout signora, the artist's wife. He found her in the garden. Dressed in a flowing gown of some white transparent material, she lay in a hammock melting in the heat, her blue eyes staring angrily up at the blue sky.

"These men have been sent to prison," she said in broken Italian.

His legs trembled as if the island had received a heavy blow. Nevertheless he found the strength to ask:

"Have they stolen something perhaps, or murdered someone?"

"Oh no. It is simply that they are Socialists."

"What are Socialists?"

"That's politics, old man," said the signora in an expiring voice and closed her eyes.

Cecco knew that foreigners are very stupid, more stupid even than Calabrians, but he wished to know the truth about his children, and so he stood for a long while beside the signora, waiting for her to open her large languid eyes. And when at last she did, he asked, pointing with his finger at the postcard:

"Is it honest?"

"I do not know," she replied resentfully. "It is politics, I told you. Don't you understand?"

No, he did not understand. Politics was something the ministers and rich men in Rome used to make the poor pay more taxes. But his sons were workers, they lived in America and were fine fellows. What had they to do with politics?"

All night long he sat with the portrait of his sons in his hands—they looked very dark in the moonlight and the old man's thoughts grew darker still. In the morning he resolved to ask the priest. The man in the black cassock said curtly:

"Socialists are men who deny the will of God. That should be enough for you."

And as the old man turned to go, he added more sternly still: "You should be ashamed of yourself taking up with such things at your age!"

"It is well that I did not show him the portrait," thought Cecco.

A few more days went by. The old man went to the barber, an empty-headed dandy, as sturdy as a young donkey. It was said of him that for money he made love to elderly American women who came to the island avowedly to enjoy the beautiful scenery but in reality to seek adventures with poor lads.

"Good God!" exclaimed this wicked man when he read the caption and his cheeks flushed with pleasure. "Arturo and Enrico, my comrades! Oh, I congratulate you, Father Ettore, with all my heart, you and myself! Now I have two more famous countrymen. Is that not something to be proud of?"

"Don't let your foolish tongue run away with you," the old man warned him.

But the barber, waving his hands cried: "Splendid!"

"What is printed here about them?" the old man insisted.

"I cannot read what it says but I am sure that it is the truth. Poor men must be great heroes if the truth is spoken of them!"

"Hold your tongue, for goodness' sake," said Cecco and stalked off, his wooden shoes clattering violently over the stones.

He went to the Russian signor of whom it was said that he was a kind and honest man. He came in, sat down by the cot on which the signor lay slowly dying, and asked:

"What is written here of these two men?"

The Russian, narrowing his eyes which were faded and sad with illness, read the caption on the postcard in a weak voice and a warm smile lit up his face.

"Signor," the old man said to him, "you see I am very old and I shall soon be going to my Maker. When the Madonna asks me what I have done with my children I shall have to tell her the whole truth. These are my children, but I do not understand what they have done and why they are in prison?"

"You may tell the Madonna," the Russian advised him earnestly, "that your children understood well her own son's chief commandment: they loved their neighbours truly..."

The old man believed the Russian, for lies cannot be uttered in simple language, lies demand fine words and flowery phrases, and he shook the sick man's small, uncalloused hand.

"Then it is not a disgrace for them to be in prison?"

"No," said the Russian. "You know that the rich are sent to prison only when they do so much evil that it can no longer be hidden. The poor are sent to prison as soon as they yearn for a little good. You are a lucky father, let me tell you!"

And he spoke to Cecco for a long time, telling him in his thin, weak voice of what honest men were doing in this world to overcome poverty and stupidity, and all the evil and abomination that springs from stupidity and poverty...

The sun burns in the heavens like a flaming flower, it pours the golden dust of its beams on to the grey rocks, and from every chink in the stone life reaches out eagerly to the sun—the green grass and the flowers as blue as the sky. Golden sparks of sunlight flare up and die in the swollen drops of crystal dew.

As he watches every living thing about him drinking in the life-giving sunlight, as he listens to the singing of the birds busily building their nests the old man thinks of his children, those boys of his on the other side of the ocean sitting behind bars in a big city, and he thinks how bad it is for their health to be in jail, poor lads...

But then he reflects that they are in prison because they have grown up to be honest young men, as their father had been all his life—and he is content and his bronze faxe relaxes in a proud smile.

"The earth is rich, men are poor, the sun is kind, man is cruel. All my life I have thought of these things and though I did not speak to them of all this they understood their father's thoughts. Six dollars a week, that is forty lire. Oho! But they thought it too little, and twenty-five thousand others like them thought the same—it is too little for a man who wishes to live well . . ."

He is certain that the ideas he cherished in his heart have blossomed out in his children and he is very proud of the fact, but knowing how rarely men believe in the fairy-tales they themselves weave from day to day, he keeps his thoughts to himself.

Yet sometimes his great old heart overflows with thoughts of his children's future, and then he straightens his weary back, inhales deeply and mustering his failing strength shouts hoarsely out to sea, over to where his children are:

"Val-o-o!"★

And the sun laughs as it rises higher and higher over the deep waters of the sea, and the men from the vineyards above echo the old man's call:

"—o-o!"

★ Here: Courage! — *Tr.*

THE NATIVITY

IT IS SOON MIDNIGHT.

Low clouds flit across the indigo sky above the little Capri square, revealing glimpses of bright star patterns! Blue Sirius flares up and dies, and the deep sonorous voice of the organ pours forth from the open doors of the church. And all this—the racing clouds, the tremulous stars, the movement of the shadows on the walls of the buildings and the stones of the square—is like soft music.

To its solemn rhythm the whole square trembles

like a theatrical set, seeming now narrow and dark, now spacious and filled with light.

Orion spreads its magnificence over Monte Soliaro. A white cloud sits on the mountain top like a bright crown, and the steep sides of the mountain, lined with crevices, resemble some dark, ancient countenance furrowed by lofty thoughts of the world and mankind.

Up there at a height of six hundred metres, hidden now by a cloud, stands a small abandoned monastery and a small cemetery with graves like rows of flower beds beneath which lie the remains of all the monks who once dwelt there. Sometimes the grey walls of the cloister peep out through the clouds as if listening to what goes on down below.

Noisy throngs of children run about the square throwing firecrackers. Tongues of fire leap into the air, scattering myriads of red sparks over the stones. Now and again some bold hand throws a lighted firecracker high into the air, where it hisses and whirls like a frightened bat. Small dark figures dart about in all directions with shouts and laughter, there is a loud explosion and for a second the figures of the children crouched in corners are illumined by the flash, their shining eyes gleaming in the darkness.

The explosions are almost unintermittent, they drown out the laughter, the cries of fear and the clatter of wooden clogs over the resonant lava. The shadows tremble and leap, the clouds glow with the lurid reflection, and the old walls of the houses seem to smile—they remember the old folk as children and have witnessed time without number this gay and rather dangerous game the children play on Christmas Eve.

But as soon as silence returns if only for a second one hears again the solemn peal of the organ, and from below the sea answers with the muffled roar of its waves breaking on the coastal rocks and the soft whisper of the pebbles.

The bay is a goblet filled with dark, frothy wine, and around its rim sparkle the city lights—the bay's bright necklace of precious gems.

The sky over Naples has an opalescent glow, it shimmers like the aurora borealis, dozens of rockets and flares tear into it, blossom out into bouquets of coloured lights, hover motionless for an instant in a quivering cloud of light and then die out with a low rumble.

The entire semi-circle of the bay is alive with this beautiful play of fire. The white lighthouse gleams coldly out at sea and the red eye of Capo di Misena glistens. But the lights on the Procida and at the foot of Ischia are like rows of large diamonds sown on to the black velvet of the night.

Herds of white-caps move across the bay. Their melodious splash muffles the roar of the distant explosions. The organ still peals and the children laugh. But suddenly the clock on the tower chimes first four and then twelve times.

The Mass is over. The crowd pours in a colourful stream through the church doors and down the broad steps to where the red firecrackers leap and writhe. The women utter little shrieks of fear, the small boys laugh with delight. This is their holiday and no one will dare forbid them to play with the scarlet fire tonight.

What fun indeed to frighten some staid grown-up dressed in his holiday clothes; to make this despot leap about on the square, twisting and turning to avoid the firecracker which chases him with a loud hiss, spattering his boots with sparks! And this happens but once a year . . .

On this anniversary of the birth of the Infant, who loved them, the children feel themselves kings and masters of life and they make the most of these few minutes of merriment to repay the adults for a whole year of tiresome domination. How they enjoy the awkward capers of the grown-ups as they try to escape the fire, begging good-naturedly for quarter: "Basta! Hey, you young scoundrels—basta!"

Now come the zamponiari, shepherds from Abruzzi, mountain folk in short blue capes and broad-brimmed hats, their shapely legs encased in white woollen stockings criss-crossed with black straps. Two of them carry bagpipes under their capes, four others have wooden horns which produce a thin high-pitched sound.

These people come down to the island every year and live here for a whole month, praising the Lord and the Holy Mother with their lovely weird music.

It is touching to see them at dawn, standing with their hats at their feet before the statue of the Madonna, gazing in adoration at the gentle face of the Mother and playing for her that inexpressibly moving melody which someone once so aptly described as the "physical awareness of God."

Now the shepherds are hurrying to take the Infant in the manger from the house of old Paolino the carpenter, to the Church of St. Theresa.

The children run after them. The narrow street swallows up their dark figures, and in a few minutes the square is empty, but for a small crowd at the church steps waiting for the procession to appear, and the warm shadows of the clouds which slide noiselessly over the walls of buildings and the heads of the people as if caressing them.

The sea sighs. Far away on the isthmus a pine-tree, like a huge vase on a delicate stem, looms in the darkness. Sirius is now dazzlingly bright. The cloud that hovered over Monte Soliaro has disappeared and the lonely little monastery perched on the edge of the cliff and the solitary tree rising sentinel-like above it are clearly visible.

The singing of the shepherds issues in radiant waves of sound from the street archway. Hatless, hook-nosed, resembling giant birds in their dark capes, they come surrounded by a throng of children carrying lanterns on long poles, and the lanterns sway in the air, lighting up the small rotund figure and silvery head of old Paolino, the flower-filled manger he carries in his arms and the pink body of the smiling Infant Christ nestling within his tiny hands uplifted in blessing.

The old man gazes at this terracotta image with such adoration as if it were indeed alive and would bring "peace on earth and good will to all men" at sunrise.

Grey, bared heads, grave faces, eyes alight with tenderness incline toward the manger from all sides. Fireworks flare up, banishing the darkness from the square as if the dawn had suddenly broken. The children sing and shout and laugh, the grown-ups smile gently, and one feels that they too would like to leap and shout for joy if only they did not fear to appear undignified before the children.

The yellow lights of candles flutter like golden moths over the crowd, and above them in the dark-blue sky glow the stars. From another street comes another procession, little girls carrying the statue of the Madonna; and now there is more music, lights, joyous shouts and children's laughter. One is caught up wholly by the spirit of the feast.

They carry the Infant Christ into the old chapel. Services have long since ceased to be held there and it stands empty all the year round. But today its ancient walls are adorned with flowers and palm leaves, golden lemons and tangerines, and the whole interior is taken up by a large skilfully executed panneau depicting the birth of Christ.

The mountains, caves, Bethlehem and fantastic castles on the mountain tops are made of large pieces of cork. A road winds snakily down the mountain sides; sheep and goats graze on meadows. There are sparkling waterfalls made of bits of glass. A group of shepherds stand looking up at the sky where a golden star blazes; angels hover in the heavens pointing with one hand toward the star of Bethlehem and with the other to the cave where the Holy Mother, and Joseph, and the Infant, with his hands upraised to the skies are seen.

A colourful caravan of Wise Men and kings in rich attire approaches the cave, and above them soar angels with palm leaves and roses in their arms. There are long-bearded Magi on camels dressed in bright silken robes, fair-haired kings on horseback in rich brocade and luxurious wigs, curly-haired Numidians, Arabs and Jews and hundreds of other colourful fantastically garbed terracotta figures.

And around the manger Arabs in white burnouses have already opened their shops and are selling weapons, silks and sweetmeats made of wax; here too men of some unknown nationality are selling wine. Women with water-jars on their shoulders are on their way to the well, a peasant leads an ass loaded with brushwood, a crowd of people are kneeling around the Infant. And children, children everywhere.

All this mass of detail is fashioned with such skill and artistry that the whole picture seems to be alive with sound and movement.

The children stand before the picture scrutinizing it closely, their sharp little eyes noticing every new detail added since the previous year. They hasten to share their discoveries with one another, arguing and laughing and shouting. And the proud artists nearby listen not without pleasure to the praise of these young connoisseurs.

True, they are grown men, fathers of families, far

too serious to be interested in playthings and they pretend that all this does not concern them. But children are often much wiser than grown-ups and always more sincere, they know that even old men like to be praised, and so they are lavish with their praise, and the artists stroke their whiskers and beards to hide their smiles of satisfaction.

Here and there the children gather in groups and confer earnestly among themselves. They are forming "bands," and on New Year's Eve they will roam over the island with Christmas Tree and Star, singing to the rattle-banging din of some ancient instruments, the jolly pagan ditties that local poets compose for the occasion every year.

> *A Happy New Year,*
> *Signor and Signora!*
> *Hear the glad tidings*
> *Your little friends bring you!*
>
> *Open your ears and hearts*
> *Open your purses,*
> *For today we rejoice,*
> *Today is Lord's day!*
>
> *Our Saviour was born,*
> *Naked and poor,*
> *The oxen warmed him*
> *With their kind, soft breath.*

> *He perished to save us*
> *From all our sorrows,*
> *And he gave his whole life*
> *For us, the poor.*

> *Praise, then, the Lord,*
> *Rejoice in his name,*
> *Make this His day*
> *A feast of joy.*

And while one band of children sings and dances to this pagan hymn, another drowns out the singing with a song merrier still:

> *Remember the shepherds,*
> *The kings and the wizards*
> *Who knelt them all*
> *Before His manger!*

Boom! boom! go the drums, while some reedy fife cannot keep pace with the children's singing and whistles along on a plaintive note:

> *And the wicked King Herod*
> *In fear of the Infant*
> *Had all little boys*
> *In the kingdom slain!*

> *But that is long past*
> *Herod is dead, and we are alive;*
> *None but capons and hens*
> *Are slain on this day.*

The grown-ups too are unable to resist the gay rhythm of the song, and now Carlo Bambola, the fat cabbie, waddles up to the children and drowning out their voices begins to sing at the top of his voice, his face red with the effort:

> *Banish all cares,*
> *Forget all sorrows.*
> *No illness shall visit,*
> *No evil befall us!*
>
> *See how the stars*
> *Light up the heavens,*
> *May our lives too*
> *Be warm and bright!*

The dark eyes of the women glow dreamily as they watch the children. The merrymaking increases, faces glow. Girls dressed in their holiday best smile coyly at the lads. The stars fade. And from somewhere up above—from the roofs or from a window—comes a ringing tenor voice:

> *Be ye healthy and gay,*
> *And all else will be well!*

The old chapel rings ever louder with the laughter of children, the finest music there is on earth. The sky over the island grows pale. Dawn is approaching. The stars recede farther and farther into the blue depths of the sky.

Amid the dark green gardens of the island golden oranges begin to glow, yellow lemons peep out of the gloom like the eyes of giant owls. The young yellowish-green shoots light up the crowns of the orange-trees. The olive leaves gleam silvery and the tracery of naked vines quivers.

The vivid carnations and the red sprigs of sage smile to the dawn. The heavy fragrance of narcissus floats on the fresh morning air, mingling with the salty breath of the sea.

The lapping of the waves grows louder, they are transparent now and their foam is as white as snow.

NUNCIA

San giacomo quarter is justly proud of its fountain. The immortal Giovanni Boccaccio loved to linger in lively discourse beside it, and it was painted more than once on the large canvases of the great Salvator Rosa, the friend of Tommaso Aniello, or Mazaniello as he was called by the poor folk for whose freedom he fought and died. Mazaniello too was born in our quarter.

Indeed many famous people were born and brought up there; in the olden days famous people were born more often than they are now and they were more conspicuous. Nowadays, when everyone walks about in jackets and goes in for politics, it is hard for a man to rise above his fellows, and besides, the soul cannot grow properly when it is swaddled in newsprint.

Until last summer Nuncia too was the pride of our quarter. Nuncia was a vegetable vendor, the happiest person in the world and the belle of our corner where the sun always shines a little longer than in other parts of the town. The fountain of course is still the same as it always was, it is growing yellower with age and will long continue to delight foreigners with its droll beauty, for the marble children never grow old and never tire of their play.

But sweet Nuncia died last summer. She died on the street in the middle of a dance, and since it is not often that people die like that it is a story worth telling.

She was too gay and warm-hearted a woman to live peacefully with any husband. Her husband did not realize this for a long time and he shouted and swore, waving his hands about and threatening people with his knife, and one day he thrust the knife into somebody's side. But the police do not like such jokes and so Stefano, after serving his time in jail, went off to the Argentine: a change of air is very good for hot-tempered people.

And so at twenty-three Nuncia was left a widow with a five-year-old daughter, a pair of donkeys, a vegetable garden and a little cart, and since a light-hearted person does not need much that was quite enough for her. She knew how to work, and there were always many who were eager to help her, and when she was short of money to pay for their labour she paid with laughter, with songs and with all those other riches that are more valuable than money.

Not all the women approved of her way of life, nor all the men either, of course, but being honest at heart she not only left the married men alone but often managed to reconcile them with their wives.

"A man who falls out of love with a woman has never really loved..." she would say.

Arturo Lano, the fisherman who had studied in a seminary as a youth and had been training for the priesthood but had since strayed from the path of righteousness and floundered in the sea, the taverns and such like pleasant spots—Lano, a master of the art of inventing immodest ditties, said to her once:

"You seem to think that love is as complicated a science as theology?"

"I know nothing of science," she replied, "but I know all your songs." And she sang to Arturo, who was as fat as a barrel:

It sooner happens so as no.
It's quite a common thing,
The Virgin Mary too, begot
Her son in early Spring

He roared with laughter of course, his clever little eyes disappearing among the folds of his fat red cheeks.

Thus she lived, joyous herself and a joy to many, pleasing to all, for in time even her woman friends forgave her, realizing that a person cannot help his character, and remembering that even the saints were not always able to conquer their own nature. Besides, man is not God, and to God alone must we be faithful.

For some ten years Nuncia shone bright as a star, acknowledged by all to be the loveliest woman and the best dancer in the quarter, and had she been a virgin she would undoubtedly have been chosen queen of the market, as indeed she was in the eyes of one and all.

She was even pointed out to foreigners, and many of them would have given much to talk to her in private, but this always made her laugh heartily.

"In what language would that much washed-out signor talk to me?"

"In the language of gold coins, little fool," respectable folk assured her. But she replied:

"I have nothing to sell to strangers besides onions, garlic and tomatoes..."

At times people who sincerely wished her well sought earnestly to persuade her.

"Only a month or so, Nuncia, and you would be a rich woman! Thing it over well, and remember you have a daughter."

"No," she said firmly. "I love my body too well to insult it. I know that it is enough to do something unwillingly once to lose your self-respect for ever."

"But you don't refuse others?"

"No, not my own kind, and when I wish it."

"What do you mean your own kind?"

"People among whom I have grown up and who understand me," was her ready answer.

Nevertheless she did have one affair with a foreigner, a forest warden from England, a strange man and silent, though the spoke our language. He was young yet his hair was grey and there was a scar across his face, the face of a cutthroat with the eyes of a saint. Some said he wrote books, others maintained that he was a gambler. She even went away with him to Sicily and came back looking very thin and worn. But he could not have been wealthy, for Nuncia brought back neither money nor gifts. And she again began to live among us, as merry and eager for happiness as ever.

But one day, on some holiday, as the people were coming out of church someone remarked with surprise:

"Look! Nina is beginning to look exactly like her mother!"

It was the truth, as clear as a day in May: Nuncia's little daughter had blossomed out, as bright a star as her mother. She was only fourteen, but very tall, with luxuriant hair and proud eyes and she looked much older than her years and quite ripe for womanhood.

Nuncia herself was amazed to look at her.

"Holy Madonna! Do you want to be more beautiful than me, Nina?"

The girl smiled. "No," she replied. "Only to be as beautiful as you, that is enough for me."

For the first time a shadow appeared on the face of the light-hearted woman, and that evening she said to her friends: "Such is life! Before you have drunk but half of your glass another hand reaches out for it..."

Of course no hint of rivalry was noticeable between mother and daughter at first. The daughter behaved with modesty and caution, she looked out at the world through her long lashes and rarely opened her mouth in the presence of men. And the mother's eyes burned more avidly, and her voice rang more seductively than ever.

Men grew flushed in her presence like sails at dawn when the first ray of the sun touches them, and true enough for many a one Nuncia was the first ray of love's day, and many watched with silent gratitude as she walked down the street beside her little cart, as straight and slender as a mast, her voice echoing over the roofs of the houses. She was lovely to look at on the market-place too as she stood before the vivid-hued heap of vegetables for all the world like a painting by some great master with the white church wall as the background— her place was by the church of San Giacomo, to the left of the steps, and she died within three paces of them. Lovely she was as she stood there like a bright flame scattering her jokes, her laughter and songs—she knew thousands of them—like gay sparks over the heads of the crowd.

She knew how to dress in such a way that her clothes set off her beauty as a crystal goblet sets off good wine: the more transparent the glass the better it shows the soul of the wine, for colour always adds to the flavour and aroma, playing to the last note that glorious song without words which we drink in order to give our spirit a little of the sun's blood. Wine! Dear God, the world with all its noise and bustle would not be worth a donkey's hoof had man not the sweet opportunity to refresh his poor soul with a good glass of red wine which, like the holy Communion, purifies us of our sins and teaches us to love and forgive this world in which there is so much ugliness. Just look at the sun through your glass and the wine will tell you such tales as you ne'er dreamed of...

There stands Nuncia in the sunshine, inspiring those about her with happy thoughts and a longing to win her favour—no man can endure to remain in the background when there is a lovely woman nearby and so he tries to outdo himself. A great deal of good was done by Nuncia, many were the forces she awakened to life. Good always inspires a desire for better.

And so, more and more often now the daughter appears beside the mother, as modest as a nun, or as a dagger in a sheath. The men look and compare, and perhaps some of them begin to understand how a woman feels sometimes and how cruel life can be to her.

Time moves on, quickening its hasty steps, and in relation to time people are like the motes of dust in a sunbeam. Nuncia's thick eyebrows are more frequently knit, and at times, biting her lip, she looks at her daughter as one gambler looks at another, trying to guess what cards the other holds.

A year passed, then another and the daughter drew ever nearer to her mother and ever farther from her. Now it was quite clear to everyone that the young men did not known in which direction to cast their tender looks—at the one or the other. And Nuncia's woman friends, than whom none can wound more unerringly, began to twit her:

"Nuncia, is your daughter going to outshine you?"

But Nuncia laughed and replied: "Big stars are visible even when the moon is out."

As a mother she was proud of her daughter's beauty, as a woman she could not but envy Nina's youth, for Nina stood between her and the sun, and the mother was loth to live in the shadow.

Lano invented a new song, its first verse went thus:

> *Were I a man I'd make my girl*
> *Give birth to such a beauty,*
> *As I myself gave birth to once,*
> *I did my woman's duty!*

Nuncia did not want to sing that song. It was rumoured that Nina had told her mother more than once: "We could live better if you were more prudent."

And the day came when the daughter said to her mother:

"Mother, you put me too much in the shade. I am not a child any more and I too want to live. You have had a gay time, is it not my turn to live now?"

"What is the matter?" the mother asked but she lowered her eyes guiltily, for she knew what it was.

About that time Enrico Borbone returned from

Australia. He was a woodcutter in that wonderful land where big money was to be had for the wishing. He came home to warm himself for a while in the sun of his homeland and intended to return to the land where life was freer than at home. He was thirty-six, a jolly, bearded giant with a merry nature, and he told fascinating stories of his adventures and of life in the dense forests. Everyone thought he was telling fairy-tales, but the mother and daughter believed it all.

"I can see that Enrico likes me," said Nina. "But you flirt with him and that makes him thoughtless and spoils my chances."

"I understand," said Nuncia. "Very well, you shall have no cause to complain to the Madonna about your mother."

And she gave up this man whom everyone knew was dearer to her than many others.

But it is a well-known fact that easy victories have a way of turning the heads of the victors, especially if the victors are still very young.

Nina began to speak to her mother in a manner Nuncia had not deserved. And one day, on San Giacomo's Day it was, our holiday, when everyone was making merry and Nuncia had just danced the tarantella magnificently, her daughter remarked aloud for all to hear:

"Are you not dancing too much? At your age it might be bad for your heart..."

All who heard those insolent words spoken in a gentle voice fell silent for a moment and Nuncia cried out in anger, her hands on her slender hips:

"My heart? You are worried about my heart? Very well, child, thank you! But we shall see whose heart is stronger!"

And considering for a moment, she proposed:

"I shall race you from here to the fountain three times there and back without stopping..."

Many thought the whole thing absurd, some indeed considered it scandalous, but the majority out of respect for Nuncia supported her proposal with mock gravity, insisting that Nina accept her mother's challenge.

They chose judges and set a time limit—observing all the rules of the race. There were many men and women who sincerely wished the mother to win, gave her their blessing and exhorted the Madonna to help her and give her strength.

And now mother and daughter stood side by side, not looking at each other; the gong went, and they set off, racing along the street to the square like two large white birds, the mother wearing a red kerchief on her head, the daughter, a pale-blue one.

From the first minutes of the race it was quite clear

that the mother was both stronger and lighter on her feet than her daughter. Nuncia ran as easily gracefully as if the earth itself carried her like a mother her child. People at the windows threw flowers on to the pavements at her feet and applauded and shouted encouragement to her. After the second lap she was more than four minutes ahead of her daughter, and Nina, crushed and upset by her defeat, dropped down panting and tearful on the church steps, unable to run a third time.

Nuncia, as fresh as a cat, bent over her, laughing with the others.

"Child," she said, stroking the girl's dishevelled hair with her strong hand. "You must know that the strongest heart in play, work and love is the heart of a woman tried by life, and that comes long after the age of thirty. So don't fret, child."

And without pausing to rest after the race, Nuncia asked for the music of the tarantella again:

"Who will dance with me?"

Enrico came forward, took off his hat, made a sweeping bow to this wonderful woman, bending his head reverently before her.

Then the tambourine began the throbbing, jangling beat of the fiery dance, as intoxicating as old, dark, mellow wine. Off went Nuncia, spinning and whirling, writhing like a serpent: well did she understand this dance of passion, and it was a sheer delight to see the lithe movements of her superb indomitable body.

She danced for a long time, and she danced with many. Her partners wearied but she could not have enough, and it was past midnight when she cried out:

"Come, once more Enrico, for the last time!" And slowly began to dance with him. Her eyes widened, shining with tender promise. Then suddenly she uttered a brief cry, threw up her arms and fell to the ground as if struck down.

The doctor said she died of heart failure.

Perhaps...

CARLONE GALIARDI

THE ISLAND SLEEPS wrapped in silence. The sea too is deathly still; it is as if some mighty hand has hurled this black, queer-shaped rock from the skies into the bosom of the sea, crushing the life out of it.

Looking at the island from the sea, from where the golden arch of the Milky Way meets the dark waters, it resembles a blunt-browed beast crouched at the edge of the shore, its back arched, silently drinking the water.

These black nights of dead calm are quite common in December; nights so strangely still that one is loath to raise one's voice above a whisper lest the noise disturb something secretly brewing in the stony silence under the blue velvet of the night sky.

In hushed voices the two men seated among the chaos of rocks on the shore are conversing. One is a customs soldier in a dark uniform jacket with yellow piping and a short rifle slung at his back—he is there to prevent the peasants and fishermen from collecting the salt deposited by time in the fissures of the rocks. The other is an old fisherman, swarthy, clean-shaven like a Spaniard, with silvery sideburns and a nose as large and hooked as a parrot's.

The rocks seem wrought in silver that has been tarnished a little by the salt water.

The soldier is young and, being young, he speaks of what is nearest to his youthful heart. The old man replies lazily, at times sternly:

"Who makes love in December?" he says. "By this time of the year the children are being born..."

"Rubbish! When people are young they do not wait..."

"Well, they ought to."

"Did you?"

"I, my friend, was not a soldier. I worked and I experienced everything it is man's lot to experience in my time."

"I don't understand."

"You will, one day."

Sirius casts its blue reflection on the water not far from the shore. If you gaze at this pale light long enough you will see a cork buoy on the water as round as a human head and perfectly motionless.

"Why are you not sleeping?"

The old man throws open his old faded cape, and replies, with a cough:

"We have cast our nets here. See the buoy?"

"Yes, I see it now."

"Three days ago one of the nets was torn up."

"Dolphins?"

"In winter? No. A shark perhaps. Who knows?"

A small stone, loosened by the foot of some invisible animal, rolled down the hillside through the dry grasses and plopped noisily into the sea. The silent night pounced eagerly on the brief noise and echoed it back lovingly from its depth as if wishing to cherish the memory of it for ever.

The soldier began softly to sing a mocking ditty:

Why do old men sleep ill?
Can you guess, Umberto?
Because in their youth
They drank too much wine . . .

"Not me," growled the old man.

> *What else makes the old sleep ill?*
> *Does clever Berghito know?*
> *Because when they were young*
> *They did not love enough.*

"A good song, eh, Uncle Pasquale?"

"You will know the answer yourself when you've passed sixty. Why ask me?"

For a long time the two sat silent, in harmony with a world hushed by the night. Presently the old man took his pipe out of his mouth, knocked it against a stone and listening to the tapping, said:

"You young lads laugh well, but I doubt whether you know how to make love as they did in the old days..."

"Bah! The old story. Love is always the same. I think."

"You think! But you do not know. Up there behind the hill lives the Senzamane family. Ask them to tell you the story of Grandfather Carlo. It will be good for your wife."

"Why should I ask strangers to tell me their story when you can tell it to me yourself?"

Somewhere an invisible night bird flew by and a

curious sound, as if the dry rocks were being rubbed with a woollen cloth, stirred the air.

The darkness grew thicker, moister and warmer, the sky receded and the stars shone brighter and brighter in the silvery haze of the Milky Way.

"In the olden days woman were more highly prized..."

"Indeed? I didn't know that!"

"The menfolk often went to war..."

"Yes, and there were a great many widows..."

"Always there were pirates and soldiers, and every five years or so new rulers appeared in Naples. The women had to be kept under look and key."

"It would be well to do the same nowadays too..."

"They used to steal them like chickens..."

"More like foxes if you ask me..."

The old man fell silent and lit his pipe. A cloud of white fragrant smoke hung in the motionless air. The match flared, lighting up the dark, crooked nose and the close-clipped moustache under it.

"Well, and what then?" the soldier asked drowsily.

"Keep quiet if you want to listen."

Sirius shone with such intensity that one might have thought the proud star wished to outshine all the other heavenly bodies. The sea was spattered with gold dust and this faintly visible reflection of the sky enlivened a little the dark silent wilderness, lending it a shimmering glow. It was as if a thousand phosphorescent eyes shone out of the sea's depths.

"I am listening," said the soldier, impatient at the hurt silence of the fisherman, and the old man began to weave one of those tales that will always be listened to with interest.

"About a hundred years ago, on the top of that mountain up there where the pine-trees grow, there lived a hunchbacked old Greek named Echellani, a smuggler with a reputation for black magic. This Echellani had a son named Aristides who was a hunter, for in those days wild goats still roamed the mountain forests. The richest family here in those days were the Galiardis. Nowadays they use their grandfather's name, Senzamane. Half of the vineyards belonged to them; they owned eight wine cellars with more than a thousand barrels. In those days our white wine was valued highly even in France where, I am told, they don't know how the value of anything but wine. Those French are all gamblers and drunkards, they even gambled away their king's head to the devil."

The soldier laughed softly and as if echoing his laughter there was a splash somewhere nearby. The two pricked up their ears and peered out toward the sea where faint ripples were receding from the shore.

"That's the fish nibbling at the hooks."

"Go on..."

"Yes... The Galiardis. There were three brothers. My story is about the middle one, Carlone as he was called because of his big mouth and his thunderous voice. He had taken a fancy to the blacksmith's daughter Giulia, a very clever girl. For some reason or other their marriage had been postponed, and they waited impatiently for their wedding day. In the meantime the Greek's son, who also had his eye on Giulia, did not waste time. For a long time he had tried to win her love, but she had repulsed his advances, and so he resolved to dishonour her in the hope that Carlone Galiardi would spurn her and then he would easily win her for himself. In those days people were stricter than they are now..."

"Well, nowadays too..."

"Loose living is the amusement of the idle rich, we here are all poor men," the old man said sternly, and returning to the past, he went on:

"One day, as the girl was gathering the cut branches of the vines, the Greek's son came by and pretending to have missed his footing on the hill path behind the wall of her vineyard, stumbled and fell heavily right at her feet. She, being a good Christian, knelt down beside him to find out whether he was hurt. He groaned.

"'Giulia,' he implored weakly. 'Do not call for help,

255

I beg you. I am afraid. If your jealous betrothed should find me here beside you he will kill me. Let me rest here a while and then I shall go...'"

"Laying his head on her knees, he pretended to swoon. The frightened girl called for help, but when the people ran up, he suddenly sprang to his feet, as healthy as you please, acting as if he were greatly embarrassed and commenced loudly to protest his love for her and his honourable intentions, declaring that he would the girl's shame by marrying her—in a word he made it appear as if, wearied by her caresses, he had fallen asleep in her lap. The gullible folk believed him in spite of the girl's angry protests. They forgot that she herself had called for help. They did not know that it is in the nature of the Greek to be cunning, that the Devil himself christened the Greeks in order to confuse things for the Christians. The girl swore that the Greek lied, but he declared that she was simply ashamed to admit the truth, that she feared the heavy hand of Carlone. He convinced them, but the girl went raving mad. She snatched up stones and hurled herself at people, so they tied her up and the whole village set out for town. By this time Carlone had heard her cries, he rushed to meet her, but when they told him what had happened, he fell on his knees before the crowd, then sprang up and struck his betrothed a blow on the face with his left hand and with the right he began to strangle the Greek. The people barely managed to tear him away."

"He was a fool," growled the soldier.

"The brains of an honest man are in his heart! I told you that all this happened in the winter just a few days before the feast of the birth of the infant Jesus. On that date people make gifts to one another of their excess wine, fruits, fish and fowl; everyone gives, and of course the poorest get the most. I do not remember how Carlone learned the truth, but he found out what had really happened and on the first day of the feast Giulia's mother and father, who had not left the house even to go to church, received only one present—a small basket of pine branches and among them—the left hand of Carlone Galiardi—the hand that had struck Giulia. They rushed in horror to his place and he met them kneeling on the threshold of his house, a blood-stained rag was bound around the arm stump, and he was weeping like a child.

"'What have you done?' they asked him.

"And he replied: 'I have done what had to be done: the man who insulted my love cannot live, and I killed him. The hand that struck my innocent beloved, wronged me, and so I cut it off... All I ask now, Giulia, is that you and yours forgive me...'

"Of course they forgave him, but there is still the

law which exists also to protect scoundrels. Galiardi was sent to jail for two years for that Greek, and it cost his brothers very dearly to get him out of prison...

"Later he married Giulia and they lived happily together to a ripe old age, bringing a new name with them to the island—Senzamane, the Handless."

The old man fell silent, sucking hard at his pipe.

"I don't like that story," said the soldier. "That Carlone of yours was a savage. And in general it was stupid."

"In a hundred years from now your life too will seem stupid," said the old man solemnly, and blowing out a cloud of white smoke, he added: "That is, if anyone will remember that you lived on this earth at all..."

Again a loud splash sounded in the stillness, violent and hasty this time. The old man threw off his cape, got up quickly and disappeared as if swallowed up by the water black and still but for the light ripples near the shore tinged with blue like silvery fish scales.

YOUNG ITALY

Night in velvet garments comes softly into the town from the meadows, and the town meets her with a myriad of golden lights. Two women and a youth are walking through the fields as if they too were meeting the night, and in their wake comes the muffled roar of the city retiring to rest after the day's toil.

Three pairs of feet shuffle softly over the dark slabs of the ancient road, paved by the polyglot gangs of Roman slaves and in the warm stillness a woman's voice rings out clear and tender:

"Do not be harsh in your dealings with people..."

"Have you ever known me to be harsh. Mother?" the youth asks thoughtfully.

"You argue with too much passion."

"I love the truth passionately."

On the youth's left hands walks a girl, her wooden shoes clicking against the stones. She walks as if she were blind, her face upraised to the sky where the evening star shines full and bright and beneath it the reddish glow of the sunset and two poplars etched against the red like unlighted torches.

"Socialists are often sent to prison," says the mother with a sigh.

"It won't be always so," the son replies calmly. "It is no use..."

"Yes, but in the meantime..."

"There is no force that can destroy the young heart of the world, and never will be..."

"Those are fit words for a song, my child..."

"Millions are singing that song, Mother, and the whole world is harkening to it more and more... You yourself never used to listen to me or Paolo so patiently and kindly as you do now."

"Yes! Yes... but the strike has driven you from your native town..."

" It is too small for two of us. Let Paolo remain! But we won the strike..."

"Yes," the girl responded warmly. "You and Paolo..."

She broke off and began to laugh softly, then they all walked on for a minute or two in silence. The ruins of some building emerged from the darkness ahead of them. Over it a sweet-scented eucalyptus spread its slender branches and when the three came up to it a faint tremor rustled the branches.

"Here is Paolo," said the girl.

A tall dark figure detached itself from the ruins and came out into the middle of the road.

"Did you heart sense his presence?" asked the youth, laughing.

"Is it you?" came the man's voice like an echo.

"Yes. Here we are. You need not come any further with me. It is only a five hours' walk to Rome, and I chose to go on foot so as to collect my thoughts on the way..."

They stopped. The tall man took off his hat.

"Don't worry about your mother and sister," he said in a choking voice. "All will be well!"

"I know. Good-bye, Mother!"

She sobbed and moaned softly. Then three kisses sounded and a manly voice said: "Go home and rest, you have had a trying time. Go, and all will be well! Paolo is as much a son to you as I. Well, little sister..."

Again the kisses and the dry rustle of feet on the stones—in the watchful stillness of the night all sounds were reflected back as in a mirror.

The dark shapes enveloped in gloom merged together and could not separate for some time. Then in silence they tore themselves apart: the three moved slowly back toward the city lights, and one strode swiftly ahead to the west, where the sunset glow had faded and a myriad of stars lit up the sky.

"Farewell!" the sorrowful cry rang softly in the night.

And from afar a cheerful voice responded: "Farewell! Do not be sad, we shall soon meet again..."

The girl's wooden shoes beat hollowly on the pavement, and the young man spoke comforting words in a slightly husky voice:

"He will be all right, Donna Filomena, you may be as sure of that as of the grace of Our Lady. He has a good head and a stout heart. He knows how to love and to make others love him... And love for one's fellow men gives a man wings to soar above everything..."

The city scatters more and more of her pale lights into the darkness. The tall man's words too glow like sparks.

"A man who carries in his heart the word that

unites men the world over will always find people who will welcome him—always!"

Just outside the city walls crouched a low white tavern staring invitingly at the passers-by with the square eye of its lighted doorway. Around three small tables at the entrance dark figures were noisily making merry to the accompaniment of throbbing guitars and the metallic twang of mandolins.

The music ceased as the three came up to the door, the voices dropped lower and several of the figures rose.

"Good evening, comrades!" cried the tall man in greeting.

And a dozen voices responded fervently:

"Good evening, Paolo, comrade! Will you join us? A glass of wine?"

"No . . . thanks!"

The mother said with a sigh: "Our people love you too."

"Our people, Donna Filomena?"

"Ah, do not laugh at me. I am not a stranger to my own kind. They all love you: you and him . . ."

The tall man took the girl's arm. "All and one more," he said. "Am I right?"

"Yes," said the girl softly. "Of course."

Then the mother laughed. "Ah, my children. When

I look at you and listen to you I cannot help believing that yours will surely be a better life than ours..."

And all three disappeared down the city street, which was as narrow and shabby as the sleeve of an old, threadbare garment.

HATRED

It HAD BEEN RAINING heavily since early morning but by midday the clouds had spent themselves, their dark fabric grew threadbare, and the wind tore it into a host of filmy shreds and blew it out to the sea, where it was woven again into a dense bluish-grey mass that cast a thick shadow on the rain-calmed water.

In the east the dark sky was rent by flashes of lightning while a magnificent sun threw its blinding light over the island.

Seen from far out at sea the island must have looked

like a rich temple on a feast day; everything so radiantly clean, decked with bright flowers, and the big rain-drops glistening everywhere, like topazes on the yellowish young leaves of the vines, amethysts on the clusters of wistaria, rubies on the scarlet geraniums and like emeralds strewn in rich profusion over the grass, the green underbrush and the leaves of the trees.

The world was hushed with the stillness that comes after rain; the only sound was the gentle babble of the brook hidden amid the rocks and under the roots of the euphorbia, dewberry and fragrant, twining clematis. Down below, the sea murmured softly.

The golden shafts of the furze pointed skywards and swayed gently, weighted with moisture, which they shook noiselessly from their fantastic blossoms.

Against the lush green background, the light-purple wistaria vied with the blood-red geraniums and roses, the rusty yellow brocade of the clematis blossoms mingled with the dark velvet of the irises and gilly-flowers, and it was all so vivid and glowing that the flowers seemed to be singing like violins, flutes and passionate 'cellos.

The moist air was fragrant and as heady as old wine.

Under a grey rock, jagged and torn by blasting, the stains of oxidized iron showing in the cracks, amid grey and yellow boulders exuding the sourish smell of dynamite, four quarrymen, husky fellows in damp rags and leather sandals, sat partaking of their midday meal.

They ate slowly and heartily out of a large bowl filled with the tough meat of the octopus fried in olive oil with potatoes and tomatoes, and washed it down with red wine quaffed in turn from a bottle.

Two of the men were clean-shaven and resembled each other sufficiently to be brothers, twins even; the third was a small, bow-legged, one-eyed chap with quick nervous gestures that made him look like an old scraggy bird; the fourth was a broad-shouldered, bearded, hook-nosed man of middle age with an abundant sprinkling of grey in his hair.

Breaking off large chunks of bread, the latter smoothed out his wine-stained whiskers and thrust a piece of bread into the dark cavern of his mouth.

"That's nonsense," he was saying, his hairy jaws working methodically. "It's a lie. I haven't done anything wrong..."

His brown eyes under their thick brows had an unhappy mocking expression. His voice was heavy and gruff, his speech slow and hesitant. Everything about him—his hat, his hairy, coarse-featured face, his large hands and his dark-blue suit spattered with white rock powder—indicated that he was the one who drilled the holes in the mountainside for blasting.

His three workmates listened attentively to what he was saying; they did not interrupt him but looked up at him from time to time as if to say: "Go on..."

And he went on, his grey eyebrows moving up and down as he spoke:

"That man, Andrea Grasso, they called him, came to our village like a thief in the night; he was dressed in rags, his hat was the colour of his boots and as tattered. He was greedy, shameless and cruel. And seven years later our elders were doffing their hats to him while he barely gave them a nod. And everyone for forty miles around was in debt to him."

"Yes, there are such people," remarked the bow-legged one, sighing and shaking his head.

The narrator glanced at him.

"So you've met that kind too?" he inquired mockingly.

The old man made an eloquent gesture, the two clean-shaven men grinned in unison, the hook-nosed blaster took a draught of wine and went on, watching the flight of a falcon in the blue sky:

"I was thirteen when he hired me along with some others to haul stones for his house. He treated us worse than animals and when my pal Lukino told him so he said: 'My ass is mine while you are a stranger to me, why should I be kind to you?' Those words were like a knife-thrust to me, and from that time on I began to watch him more closely. He was mean and brutal to everybody, even the old men and women, it made no difference to him, I could see that. And when decent folk told him he was behaving badly he laughed in their faces: 'When I was poor,' he said, 'no one treated me any better.' He took up with priests, carabinieri and policemen, the rest of the people saw him only when they were in grave trouble and then he could do what he liked with them."

"Yes, there are people like that," repeated the bow-legged one softly and all three glanced at him in sympathy: one of the clean-shaven workers silently handed him the wine bottle, the old man took it, held it up to the light and before putting it to his lips, said: "I drink to the sacred heart of the Madonna!"

"He often used to say that the poor have always worked for the rich and the fools for the wise, and that is how it must be always."

The story-teller laughed and stretched out his hand for the bottle. It was empty. He threw it carelessly on to the stones alongside the hammers, picks and a coil of fuse.

"I was a youngster then and I resented those words deeply. So did my workmates, for they killed our hopes, our desire for a better life. Late one night I and Lukino my friend met him as he was crossing the field on horseback. We stopped him and said politely but firmly: 'We ask you to be kinder to folk.'"

The clean-shaven fellows burst out laughing and the one-eyed one too chuckled softly, while the narrator heaved a deep sigh:

"Yes, of course, it was stupid! But youth is honest. Youth believes in the power of the word. You might say that youth is life's conscience..."

"Well, and what did he say?" asked the old man.

"He yelled: 'Let go of my horse, you scoundrels!' And he pulled out a pistol and pointed it at us. We said: 'You have no need to fear us, Grasso. And don't be angry. We are merely giving you a piece of advice!'"

"Now that was good!" said one of the clean-shaven men, and the other nodded in agreement; the bow-legged one pursed his lips and stared at a stone, stroking it with his crooked fingers.

The meal was over. One of the men amused himself by knocking the crystalline raindrops off the blades of grass with a thin stick, another looked on, picking his teeth with a dry grass stalk. The air grew drier and hotter. The brief shadows of noon were melting rapidly. The sea murmured a gentle accompaniment to the solemn tale:

"That encounter had unpleasant consequences for Lukino. His father and uncle were in debt to Grasso. Poor Lukino grew thin and haggard, he ground his teeth and his eyes lost the brightness that had once attracted the girls. 'Ah,' he said to me once, 'that was a foolish thing we did that day. Words are worth nothing when addressed to a wolf!' 'Lukino is ready for murder,' I thought to myself. I was sorry for the lad and his good family. But I was poor myself and all alone in the world, for my mother had died shortly before."

The hook-nosed worker brushed his moustache and beard with his lime-stained fingers, and as he did so a heavy silver ring gleamed on the forefinger of his left hand.

"I might have done a service to my fellowmen if I had been able to carry the thing to the end, but I am softhearted. One day, meeting Grasso on the street, I walked alongside him and speaking as humbly as I could, said: 'You are a mean, greedy fellow, it is hard for folks to live with you, you are liable to push someone's hand and that hand may reach for a knife. My advice to you is to go away from here.' 'You're a fool, young man!' he said, but I kept insisting. 'Listen,' he said with a laugh, 'how much will you take to leave me in peace? Will a lira be enough?' That was an insult but I controlled my anger. 'Go away from here, I tell you!' I insisted. We were walking shoulder to shoulder, I on his right. When I wasn't looking he drew out his knife and stuck me with it. You can't do much with your left hand, so it went into my chest only one inch deep. Naturally I flung him to the ground and kicked him the way you would kick a hog."

"'Now perhaps you will take my advice!' I said as he writhed on the ground."

The two clean-shaven fellows threw an incredulous glance at the speaker and dropped their eyes. The bow-legged one bent over to tie the leather thongs of his sandals.

"The next morning when I was still in bed the carabinieri came and took me to the sheriff who was a pal of Grasso's. 'You are an honest man, Ciro,' he said, 'so you will not deny that you tried to murder Grasso last night.' I said that was not exactly the truth, but they have their own way of looking at things. So they kept me in jail for two months before I was brought to trial and then they sentenced me to a year and eight months. 'Very well,' I told the judges, 'but that isn't the end of it!' "

He drew a fresh bottle from its cache among the stones and thrusting it under his moustaches took a long draught of the wine; his hairy Adam's apple moved thirstily up and down and his beard bristled. Three pairs of eyes watched him in grave silence.

"It's boring to talk about it," he said handing the bottle to his workmates and smoothing his moist beard.

"When I returned to the village I saw there was no room for me there; everyone was afraid of me. Lukino told me that things had got even worse that year. He was sick to death of it all, the poor lad. 'Very well,' I said to myself and went to see that man Grasso. He was terribly scared when he saw me. 'Well, I'm back,' I said. 'Now it's your turn to go away!' He snatched up his rifle and fired but it was loaded with bird shot and he aimed at my legs. I didn't even fall. 'Even if you had killed me I would come and haunt you from the grave,' I told him. 'I have sworn to the Madonna that I shall get you out of here. You are stubborn, but so am I.' We got into a scuffle and before I knew it I had accidentally broken his arm. I hadn't intended to do him violence and he had attacked me first. A crowd gathered and I was taken away. This time I got three years and nine months and when my term ended, the warden, who knew the whole story and liked me, tried hard to persuade me not to go back home. He offered me a job with his son-in-law who had a big plot of land and a vineyard in Apulia. But I, naturally, could not give up what I had undertaken. So I went home, this time firmly resolved not to indulge in any useless chatter, for I had learned by then that nine words out of ten are superfluous. I had only one thing to say to him: 'Get out!' I arrived in the village on a Sunday and went straight to Mass. Grasso was there. As soon as he saw me he jumped up and yelled all over the church: 'That man has come here to kill me, citizens, the devil has sent him for my soul!' I was surrounded before I had time to touch him, before I had time to tell him what I wanted. But it didn't matter for he fell on to the stone floor in a fit and his right side and his tongue were paralyzed. He died seven weeks later ... That's all. And folks invented a sort of legend about me. Very terrible, but a lot of nonsense."

He chuckled, looked up at the sun and said:

"Time to get started ..."

In silence the other three rose slowly to their feet; the hook-nosed worker stared at the rusty, oily cracks in the rock and said: "Let's get to work ..."

The sun was at its zenith and all the shadows had shrivelled up and vanished.

The clouds on the horizon sank into the sea whose waters had grown calmer and bluer than before.

PEPE

Pᴇᴘᴇ ɪs ᴛᴇɴ, he is as frail, slender and quick as a lizard, his motley rags hang from his narrow shoulders, and the skin, blackened by sun and dirt, peeps through innumerable rents.

He looks like a dried-up blade of grass, which the sea breeze blows hither and thither. From sunrise to sunset Pepe leaps from stone to stone on the island and hourly one can hear his tireless little voice pouring forth:

> *Italy the Beautiful,*
> *Italy my own!*

277

Everything interests him: The flowers that grow in riotous profusion over the good earth, the lizards that dart among the purple boulders, the birds amid the chiselled perfection of the olive-tree leaves and the malachite tracery of the vines, the fish in the dark gardens at the sea bottom and the foreigners on the narrow, crooked streets of the town: the fat German with the sword-scarred face, the Englishman who always reminds one of an actor in the role of a misanthrope, the American who endeavours in vain to look like an Englishman, and the inimitable Frenchman as noisy as a rattle.

"What a face!" Pepe remarks to his playmates, with his keen eyes at the German who is so puffed out with importance that his very hair seems to stand on end. "Why, he's got a face as big as my belly!"

Pepe doesn't like Germans, he shares the ideas and sentiments of the streets, the squares and the dark little saloons where the townsfolk drink wine, play cards, read the papers and discuss politics.

"The Balkan Slavs," they say, "are much closer to us poor southerners than our good allies who presented us with the sands of Africa in reward for our friendship."

The simple folk of the south are saying this more

and more often and Pepe hears everything and forgets nothing.

Here is a dull Englishman, striding along on his scissor-like legs. Pepe in front of him is humming something like a funeral dirge or just a mournful ditty:

> My friend has died,
> My wife is sad . . .
> And I do not know
> What ails her.

Pepe's playmates trail along behind convulsed with laughter, scurrying like mice to hide in the bushes or behind walls whenever the foreigner glances at them calmly with his faded eyes.

One could tell a host of entertaining stories about Pepe.

One day some signora sent him to her friend with a basket of apples from her garden.

"I will give you a soldo!" she said, "You can well use it."

Pepe readily picked up the basket, balanced it on his head and set off. Not until evening did he return for the soldo.

"You were in no great hurry," the woman remarked.

"Ah, dear signora, but I am so tired!" Pepe replied with a sigh. "You see there were more than ten of them!"

"Why, of course, there were more than ten! It was a full basket!"

"Not apples, signora, boys."

"But what about the apples?"

"First the boys, signora: Michele, Giovanni. ."

The woman grew angry. She seized Pepe by the shoulder and shook him:

"Answer me, did you deliver the apples?" she cried.

"I carried them all the way to the square, signora! Listen how well I behaved. At first I paid no attention to their jibes. Let them compare me to a donkey, I told myself, I will endure it all out of respect for the signora, for you, signora. But when they began to poke fun at my mother, I decided I had had enough. I put the basket down and you ought to have seen, good signora, how neatly I pelted those little devils with those apples. You would have enjoyed it!"

"They stole my fruit!" cried the woman.

Pepe heaved a mournful sigh.

"Oh, no," he said, "the apples that missed were smashed against the wall, but the rest we ate after I had beaten my enemies and made peace with them..."

The woman loosed a flood of abuse on Pepe's small shaven head. He listened attentively and humbly, clicking his tongue now and again in admiration at some particularly choice expression. "Oho, that's a beauty! What a language!"

And when at last her anger had spent itself and she left him, he shouted after her:

"You wouldn't have felt that way if you saw how beautifully I swatted the filthy heads of those good-for-nothings with those wonderful apples of yours. If only you could have seen it, why you'd have given me two soldi instead of one!"

The silly woman did not understand the modest pride of the victor, she merely shook her fist at him.

Pepe's sister who was much older, but not smarter than he, went to work as housemaid in a villa owned by a rich American. Her appearance altered at once; she became neat and tidy, her cheeks became rosy, and she began to bloom and ripen like a pear in August.

"Do you really eat every day?" her brother once asked her.

"Twice and three times a day if I wish," she replied proudly.

"See you don't wear out your teeth," Pepe advised.

"Is your master very wealthy?" he inquired after a pause.

"Oh, yes, I believe he is richer than the king!"

"You can't fool me! How many pairs of trousers has he got?"

"Hard to say."

"Ten?"

"More, perhaps..."

"Then bring me a pair, not too long in the leg but the warmest you can find," said Pepe.

"What for?"

"Well, just look at mine!"

There was indeed not much to see, for little enough remained of Pepe's trousers.

"Yes," his sister agreed, "you really need some clothes! But won't he think we have stolen them?"

"Don't imagine that folks are sillier than we are!" Pepe reassured her. "When you take a little from someone who has a lot, that isn't stealing, it's just sharing."

"You're talking nonsense," his sister objected, but Pepe soon overcame her scruples and when she came into the kitchen with a good pair of light-grey trousers, which were, of course, far too large for Pepe he knew at once how to overcome that difficulty.

"Give me a knife!" he said.

Together they quickly converted the American's trousers into a very convenient costume for the boy; the result of their efforts was a somewhat loose, baggy but not uncomfortable sack attached to the shoulders by bits of string that could be tied around the neck, with the trouser pockets serving as sleeves.

They might have turned out an even better and more convenient garment had the wife of the owner of the trousers not interrupted their labours. She came into the kitchen and began to give vent to a string of very ugly words in many languages, pronounced equally badly, as is customary with Americans.

Pepe could do nothing to check the flow of eloquence; he frowned, pressed his hand to his heart, clutched despairingly at his head and sighed loudly, but she did not calm down until her husband appeared on the scene.

"What's up?" he asked.

Whereupon Pepe spoke up:

"Signor, I am greatly astonished by the commotion your signora has raised, in fact I am somewhat offended for your sake. As far as I can see she thinks that we have spoiled the trousers, but I assure you that they are just right for me! She seems to think that I have taken your last pair of trousers and that you cannot buy yourself another pair..."

The American, who had listened imperturbably to the speech, now remarked:

"And I think, young man, that I ought to call the police."

"Really," Pepe queried in amazement, "what for?"

"To take you to jail..."

Pepe was extremely hurt. In fact, he was ready to weep, but he swallowed his tears and said with great dignity:

"If, signor, it gives you pleasure to send people to jail, that is your affair! But I would not do that if I had many pairs of trousers and you had none! I would give you two, perhaps even three pairs; although it is impossible to wear three pairs of trousers at once! Especially in hot weather..."

The American burst out laughing, for even rich men can sometimes see a joke. Then he treated Pepe to some chocolate and gave him a franc piece. Pepe bit at the coin and thanked the donor:

"Thank you, signor! The coin is genuine, I presume?"

But Pepe is at his best when he stands alone somewhere among the rocks, pensively examining their cracks as if reading the dark history of rock life. At such moments his vivid eyes are dilated and filmy with wonder, his slender hands are laced behind his back and his head, slightly bent, sways a little from side to side like a flower in the breeze. And under his breath he softly hums a tune, for he is for ever singing.

It is good also to watch him looking at flowers, at the wistaria blossoms that pour in purple profusion over the walls. He stands as taut as a violin string as if he were listening to the soft tremor of the silken petals stirred by the breath of the sea breeze.

As he looks he sings: "Fiorino... Fiorino..."

And from afar, like the sound of some huge tambourine, comes the muffled sigh of the sea. Butterflies chase one another over the flowers. Pepe raises his head and follows their flight, blinking in the sunlight, his lips parted in a smile tinged a little with envy and sadness, yet the generous smile of a superior being on earth.

"Cho!" he cries, clapping his hands to frighten an emerald lizard.

And when the sea is as placid as a mirror and the rocks are bare of the white lacy spume of the tide, Pepe, seated on a stone, gazes with his bright eyes into the transparent water where among the reddish seaweed the fish glide smoothly, the shrimps dart back and forth and the crab crawls along sideways.

And in the stillness the clear voice of the boy pours gently forth over the azure waters:

"Sea, oh, Sea..."

Adults often shake their heads disapprovingly at Pepe, saying: "That one will be an anarchist!"

But kinder folk, possessed of greater discernment, are of a different opinion:

"Pepe will be our poet..."

And Pasqualino, the cabinet-maker, an old man with a head seems cast in silver and a face like those etched on ancient Roman coins—wise and respected Pasqualino has his own opinion:

"Our children will be far better than we, and their lives will be better too!"

Many folk believe him.

EASTER

Through the gloom of a moonless Saturday before Easter a woman shrouded in black slowly made her way through the narrow slits of alleys in the town's outskirts. The hood over her head hid her face from view, and the ample folds of the loose cape made her look inordinately tall; she walked in silence, the very personification of the uttermost depths of sorrow.

Behind her, at the same slow peace, came the musicians—a group so compact as to seem like a single body—and above them floated the awesome brass mouths of their instruments, some extended forward, others raised up to the black sky, and all blaring, groaning: the clarinets sang their doleful song like so many monks at the end of a long, sleepless vigil, and the bassoon recalled an ill wind moaning in the eaves; the cornet-à-piston added its raucous wail and was echoed by the despodent French horns; the saxhorn intoned its sorrowful chant and the big drum beat out the measure of the sombre march, while the dry rat-a-tat of the little drum merged with the shuffling of hundreds of feet over the paving stones.

The brass gleamed with a yellow, lifeless lustre, the men caught in its toils looked like some strange monsters from another world, and the wood winds jutted out snout-like from the knot of musicians forming the head of the enormous black snake that slithered painfully through the narrow streets of grey-walled houses.

Every now and then this strange procession poured into one of the tiny, irregular squares that look so much like holes worn by time in the stone garb of the city, and then squeezed once more into the narrow slit of a street as if in a vain effort to force its walls apart. Hour after hour the sinister serpent, each of whose segments was a living human body, crawled through the city under the silent dome of the heavens, following the mysterious figure of the woman.

Silent, black-garbed, encased in an impenetrable armour of sorrow, she continued her quest in the gloom of night, carrying the imagination of the spectator deep into the darkness of ancient beliefs, reminding one of Isis whose brother and husband fell victim to the evil Seth, until her strange figure seemed to emanate an aura of blackness that immersed everything around in the murk of long ago revived this night in order to impress on man his bond with the past.

The funereal strains echoed against the windows, sending tremors through the glass, yet the sound of the music and the low murmur of voices was muted by the shuffling of thousands of feet against the paving stones. The stones were hard underfoot, yet the earth seemed shaky and the world small, a heavy smell of humanity hung over it, and one's eyes kept turning to the sky where the stars glowed dimly through a pall of mist.

But now a red reflection of light gleamed on the black rectangles of windows on a high wall in the distance—gleamed, disappeared, flashed again, and a suppressed murmur passed through the throng as a spring breeze through forest thickets:

"They're coming . . . They're coming . . ."

Somewhere ahead new sounds had been born and were now gaining in volume—sounds less sombre, and the light there was growing brighter too. The woman seemed to have quickened her steps and the crowd surged forward at a livelier pace to keep up with her, even the musicians missed a beat and for a moment the melody faltered, its pattern broken; a hasty flute piped a false high note, evoking a ripple of soft laughter.

The next moment, with the unexpectedness of a fairy-tale, a small square opened up ahead with two figures lit up by torches and Bengal lights in the middle. One was the familiar fair-haired figure of Christ in flowing white robes, and the other, his favourite disciple, John, in a blue tunic. Around them milled dark shapes with flaming torches in their hands, their swarthy southern features illuminated by a smile of sublime joy—joy they themselves had conjured into being and exulted in.

Christ too was in gay spirits. With one hand he held the instrument of his death decked in flowers, and with the other he gesticulated as he spoke. John, young, beardless, handsome as Adonis, threw back his head with the flowing curls and laughed.

The crowd spilled on to the square and formed

a circle around the two, while the woman, black as cloudy night, seemed to rise and float up to Christ. On reaching him she stopped and threw back her hood, and her black shroud settled cloud-like to her feet.

In the gay, exultant light of the flickering torches the falling hood revealed the radiant, golden head of the Madonna, and from under her cloak and from the hands of the figures closest to the Mother of God scores of white doves rose with flashing wings to the dark sky. Indeed, for a moment it seemed that the woman garbed in white gleaming with silver and garlanded with flowers, the white, almost transparent Christ and the blue John—all three figures of a mien so strange and unearthly—floated to heaven in the living flutter of the dove's wings as if surrounded by Cherubims. "Gloria, Madonna, gloria!" the cry from a thousand throats rose from the dark mass of the throng and the world underwent a magic transformation: lights blazed in all the windows, uplifted arms raised torches over the heads of the crowd, golden sparks showered down everywhere, green, red and purple lights burst forth, the pigeons wheeled overhead and all faces were turned up as the crowd shouted in rapture:

"Gloria, Madonna, gloria!"

The walls of the houses trembled in the play of light and children and women, both young and old, appeared in all the windows. Their bright-coloured holiday garb blossomed out like enormous flowers, while the silver-robed Madonna, standing between John and Christ, seemed to be aflame and melting away—one now saw she had large pink-and-white features, huge eyes, a crown of golden hair falling in two luxuriant cascades of fine curls to her shoulders. Christ was laughing gaily as befits the resurrected and the blue-eyed Madonna smiled and shook her head as John seized a torch and waved it, scattering sparks around him—he was still a mere boy, sharp-eyed, lithe and agile like a bird, and evidently enjoyed a prank.

All three laughed infectiously as only those can laugh who dwell under the southern sun, on the shores of the merry sea, and looking at them, the people around laughed too—these people who know how to make merry, who have the gift of creating beauty out of everything, and who themselves are the most beautiful spectacle of all.

The children were there of course. They fluttered about at the feet of the three figures just as the white birds fluttered in the air above them, shouting in their resounding, gay, excited voices:

"Gloria, Madonna, gloria!"

The old women were praying. They looked at the trinity as lovely as a dream, and although they knew very well that the Christ was a carpenter from the via Pisacane, John, a watch-maker, and the Madonna, none other than the gold-embroiderer Anita Bragaglia, they prayed, whispering with their withered lips warm words of gratitude to the Madonna for everything, and most of all for existing ...

The sound of solemn singing carried from the distance and the words of the old familiar song came to mind:

"Of death we celebrate the death ..."

Day was breaking. The gaily ringing church bells vied with one another to proclaim that Christ, the God of Spring, had risen from the dead. In the square the musicians closed ranks and music blared forth, and in step with it many moved on toward the churches where the organs were also singing deep-throated praises to the resurrected God of Spring and a multitude of birds, brought along by people to be released at this solemn moment, were flitting under the domes.

It is a grand tradition, this custom of making birds, the purest of all living creatures, a party to man's finest fête; a wondrous melody fills the heart at the sight of these hundreds of tiny winged beings in their multi-coloured plumage flying about the church, twittering, trilling, perching on the cornices and statues, flitting every now and then down to the altar.

The square grew deserted. The three radiant figures had started some melodious song and walked down the street arm in arm, followed by the musicians, and these by the throng. The children scampered after them looking in the light of the multi-coloured festive illumination like so many coral beads broken off their string. As for the pigeons, they had perched on the roof tops and eaves and were cooing.

And again the words of the good old song came to mind:

"Christ is arisen..."

And we all shall rise from the dead, invoking death upon death.

ERRATA

	Reads	Should read
p. 12, 11 line from top	seemed to reveberate	seemed to reverberate
p. 20, 11 line from top	spread is heavy	spread in heavy
p. 23, 5 line from bottom	straightened his at, and, walked off	straightened his hat, and walked off
p. 36, 10 line from bottom	that we dare not to.	that we dare not do.
p. 56, 2 line from bottom	for you weakness!	for your weakness!
p. 81, 9 line from top	"She is made!"	"She is mad!"
p. 108, 1 line from bottom	how everyone loved three	how everyone loved thee
p. 109, 7 line from bottom	who knew better than she were	who knew better than she where
p. 134, 1 line from top	"It was born	"I was born
p. 146, 11 line from top	attention to this expect his sister;	attention to this except his sister;
p. 153, 13 line from top	head on her fingers.	head or her fingers.
p. 178, 8 line from top	but first the took	but first she took
p. 185, 4 line from bottom	Insolence du think?	Insolence you think?

	Reads	Should read
p. 217, 8 line from top	It most cases	In most cases
p. 221, 6 line from bottom	bronze faxe relaxes	bronze face relaxes
p. 239, 4 line from top	Thing it over	Think it over
p. 239, 11 line from bottom	though the spoke	though he spoke
p. 246, 2 line from top	easily gracefully	easily and gracefully
p. 253, 6 line from top	woman were	women were
p. 253, 13 line from top	to be kept under look	to be kept under lock
p. 254, 7 line from bottom	know how the value	know now the value
p. 256, 9 line from top	that he would the girl's	that he would hide the girl's
p. 260, 5 line from top	On the youth's left hands	On the youth's left hand
p. 262, 12—13 lines from bottom	on the payement	on the pavement
p. 287, 2 line from bottom	the same slow peace,	the same slow pace,
p. 288, 8 line from top	by the despodent	by the despondent